BATTLE EARTH VIII

NICK S. THOMAS

ISBN 978-1-911092-02-5

Typeset by Swordworks Books
Printed and bound in the UK & US
A catalogue record of this book is available
from the British Library

Cover design by Swordworks Books
www.swordworks.co.uk

BATTLE EARTH VIII

NICK S. THOMAS

PROLOGUE

Life in peacetime hadn't been what Mitch Taylor had either expected or hoped for, but it wasn't to last anyway. Four years of lying idle as a propaganda puppet had built his appetite for action, but that also came in a form he could not have anticipated.

War had been declared by one group of humans against another. The kind of war Taylor was all too familiar with in history books but had zero experience in the real world. Tsengal's revelation about the Krys agents living among them had resulted in his death before the proof of such could save them from a new world war.

It had been a month since war had been declared by the European Alliance against their former colleagues in the Union of European Nations. The rest of the world was yet to pick sides, and neither had made any determined attempt to cross one another's borders.

A great war was coming, and all the time the threat loomed over them from the alien invaders. The threat of Erdogan, a grand leader of the alien forces Taylor only knew by reputation. But for now, all Taylor could do was face what was in front of him.

CHAPTER ONE

Taylor sat inside the remnants of a stone building that had recently been demolished after having clearly stood for hundreds of years. He couldn't make out what it used to be, as there was little left to identify. A road sign lay across the rubble beside him; it was in German and meant little to him.

"Damn thing nearly took my fucking head off," he stated.

Grey grunted in response without even looking up at him. He'd just heated water on a stove and was busy pouring the hot liquid into a mug.

"Not one of you can go a half hour without a cup of tea, can you?" Taylor continued. "Random road sign could have killed me, but no never mind, your tea is more important."

"Huh?" he asked, as he finally finished making the tea

and looked over in surprise, having clearly not listened to a word.

"No matter," responded Taylor. "I don't know why you insist on boiling the water yourself. Our flasks will do the job in ten seconds without all the fuss. And you still carry tea bags around with you? You're an anachronism, Captain."

He smiled in response.

"Dear Colonel, there is far more to enjoying a cup of tea than merely pouring it down your throat."

Grey lifted the mug to his mouth, and Taylor could not help but be amused by the look of content and concentration on his face as he did so. But as the folded edge of the mug met with the Captain's lips, a cry rang out from nearby.

"Incoming!"

Before either of them could react, an explosion ripped through an adjacent building and sent dust and debris hurtling through the air. In the moment of silence after the blast, Taylor looked back to Grey who sat precisely where he had been and still holding his mug. He was covered in a thick grey cloud of dust, looking in disgust at his freshly made beverage floating with dirt. Taylor couldn't help but laugh.

"Shit!" Grey swore, throwing down the mug in disgust; his further expletives drowned out by a barrage that engulfed their position, forcing him to jump for cover. He landed down in a crater they had expanded into a trench.

"See, you could have drunk it by now if you'd used the flask!" yelled Taylor.

"That's a big help!"

Explosions hit all around their position but to little effect with the deep dugouts they had created. Taylor looked at his watch and counted the minutes to when the firing stopped.

"Three minutes."

"Same shit, different day," replied Grey.

He stumbled out of the trench; satisfied in the knowledge the attack was over, shook as much dust off as he could and picked up his mug, looking at it in disgust.

"Have to start all over again."

Taylor ignored him and carried on with his own train of thought. "That sign must have been blown a few clicks to have got here, this side of the border."

"Yeah, or it was dragged here by a vehicle a few years back, or collected as a memento from whoever occupied this place. Maybe they stole it and put it up on display in their office?"

"Now you're just making shit up."

"Well there are few certainties here, aren't there? Except for the fact they bomb us for three minutes every six hours, which seems pointless in itself as they aren't following it up with anything."

Taylor stood up tall over the wreckage as Grey continued

to curse and tried to wash out his precious mug. "You spoke too soon."

Grey looked up and was surprised to see Taylor's face was deadly serious.

"Down!" he shouted. He jumped down onto Grey, causing the mug to fly from his hands. A second after they hit the scattered debris, an explosion erupted above them on one of the remaining walls. As the dust settled, the two rolled over into their trench once again, the gunfire intensifying.

"That's no artillery," said Grey.

"No, an armoured column."

"I don't see how that's our problem."

"It is once they're on top of us."

Taylor crept to the edge of the trench to look over cautiously at the wide expanse before them. The small town they had occupied was in the middle of a broad flat plain, with little cover except for the remains of the buildings and those defences they had dug themselves. Grey joined him. As they looked out, a couple of marines jumped in behind them.

"We got half the German army coming down the road, Colonel!"

He didn't respond but studied the scene around them. A dozen armoured vehicles had come up over the crest a klick ahead, and more were pouring over.

"Never thought I'd see it," he muttered.

"What?" Grey asked.

"A conventional army coming at us, a human army."

"I don't think that's all it is," replied Grey, studying the incoming forces.

From between the vehicles, they spotted Mechs swarming over the crest towards them and using the vehicles for cover.

A volley of their own guns thundered across the plain and hit the incoming forces. Three tanks burst into flames, and the bodies of Mech soldiers were thrown into the air.

"How can they not see this is wrong?" asked Grey.

"God knows how many humans on that side are even still actually human. There are forces at work here which are forcing us to fight each other."

"What are we gonna do about it?"

"What do you do when someone attacks you, Captain?"

"Fight back."

"Sure, then you have your answer."

"But... those are people, not aliens."

"And now they're the enemy, and they'll blow your head off if you don't do the same to them first. Remember that, Captain. They might all as well be Krys as far as we're concerned."

A burst of shots rushed over their heads, forcing the two of them to duck down.

"A broad daylight attack, they're getting pretty ambitious, aren't they?" yelled Grey.

Taylor looked back at the sweeping advance heading their way.

"Maybe they got a right to be."

He turned back to see Jafar had reached their position, but he had not heard him coming, though it was hard to hear anything over the gunfire.

"You see that, mate," said Grey to him. "A few thousand of your kind, and they're coming for you."

"They're coming for all of us," replied Taylor. "All right, get the RATs ready."

Jafar looked confused by the term.

"Reitech Anti-tank. Latest baby in the arsenal," replied Grey, turning away to radio in the orders.

Jafar looked over to the next trench as the orders were relayed and could see one of the troops lifting up a shoulder-mounted weapon. It looked like little more than a pipe with handles.

"Reiter's latest toy," added Taylor. "I'm told it'll take out all but the heaviest Krys armour from half a klick, so God knows what it'll do to our own vehicles."

"I've been waiting to see these in action all year," stated Grey.

Taylor could see the genuine excitement in his face, and it amused him that in the face of such danger he could be so. "Fire when ready," ordered Taylor. "Fire when ready," relayed Grey over the comms.

They watched intently just far enough above the trench

edge to get a view without becoming targets themselves. The closest RAT fired, and a burst of blue light flashed out the rear tube that was hot enough it scorched the ground around the user.

The projectile soared across the potholed and dusty battlefield and struck the front armour of one of the incoming tanks almost centre at the hull. The light seemed to pass right through the armour and blast the turret clean into the air. It hurtled off into a number of the Mechs, wreaking further destruction as the tank ground to a halt and smoke began pouring from it when it caught fire.

"Holy shit!" yelled one of the nearby marines.

It was a relief the equipment they had been issued with actually worked, but a horrific sight to endure when they all knew fellow humans were inside the tank; humans they had so recently fought beside. They all still failed to comprehend how mankind could stand with the enemy, but there seemed little they could do but fight back now.

"Fire at will!" Taylor ordered over the comms.

Pulses of the RAT launchers continued to soar across the battlefield as quickly as they could be reloaded. They seemed to make light work of the armoured vehicles, and yet still they came. Taylor took aim at the first Mech he could spot and fired. The target vanished between vehicles and smoke as he pulled the trigger, leaving him no idea if the shot had met its target. He moved onto the next and could see the rest of the Regiment were doing the same.

A moment later they caught a few dozen Mechs in the open where their covering vehicles had been destroyed and all hell was unleashed on them. Those that were in plain sight were cut down in seconds, but the armoured advance continued. As vehicle after vehicle was disabled, he wondered how the crews could muster the courage to continue on.

"They aren't stopping!" Grey shouted.

They could hear their comrades' rate of fire increase rapidly as the defence became more desperate. The artillery fire at their backs continued smashing the enemy advance, but they knew that they'd be under the guns soon enough. Mitch slammed in a new magazine and kept up the fire at the Mechs that were rushing towards them. They seemed as unstoppable as ever. A vehicle ahead swerved, and as it was struck, a dozen Mechs came out from behind and stormed forward to their position. He turned his rifle on the nearest and gunned it down while his comrades tried frantically to do the same.

Four of the creatures reached the edge of the trench, and Mitch pulled the trigger as one came at him gun at the ready, to find the last round he had glanced off the alien's shoulder. He pulled his shield from the trench side to cover himself just in time as a burst of automatic fire struck. Before he could reach for his Assegai, the beast jumped on top of him. The weight forced his shield to smash down onto him. The impact shocked his head and only his helmet saved it from being crushed.

Unable to respond, Taylor felt a hard wrench. The alien soldier tried to prise the shield from him like it was ripping a shell of a turtle. He held on firm and was lifted and thrown up into the air, but because the creature held on, he couldn't keep hold and was launched out of the trench towards the enemy assault.

Mitch hit the ground hard and rolled several times until he came to an abrupt halt and crashed into the legs of one of the Mechs. It stumbled slightly as it lost balance and rolled over just narrowly missing landing on his legs. To his side he could see the bodies of several fallen enemy soldiers and tracers zipped overhead. He knew he had just a few seconds to get to his feet, and he did exactly that.

As he jumped up, he drew his Assegai but could not help but feel naked without a rifle or shield. He quickly glanced in all directions to get his bearings and stopped when he saw a rifle being aimed at him. His instincts kicked in, and he leapt to the side and rolled as the gunfire flew past, but he'd leapt into the path of another danger, a Mech soldier. He ducked as it swung its rifle toward him with all its crushing weight, but he was done being on the defensive.

As Taylor arose from his crouched position, his Assegai too drove upwards into the stomach of the Mech armour. The creature groaned in pain and again swung at him, but he leapt back out of the way. Then it came right back, and he plunged thrust down into the faceplate of its armour. The strike caused the beast to immediately freeze where it stood and then to topple over with the weight of the Colonel against it.

For a moment Taylor felt glad to have survived once more, but then he remembered the danger they were in and the realisation he stood out in plain view on the open plain. He was almost in a daydream and still stunned, but his hearing was coming back. He could hear his people yelling from the trench.

"Get back! Colonel, get back!" they screamed.

Finally, he felt a hand on his shoulder, and it yanked him around hard. He was met by the face of Jafar which first made his pulse pound, as the sight of an alien up close and personal always did, but Jafar said nothing. His alien friend only studied him until he finally snapped out of it and stood up. He turned back to the battlefield to look at the result of their work and the terrible devastation.

"Colonel, get to cover!" Grey hollered.

Taylor shook his head and looked at the wreck of the armoured vehicle that had reached the farthest point. It was just twenty metres from where he stood. As he began to pace towards it, the pitch and volume of the Captain's voice increased, but he ignored them. Jafar followed out of curiosity. They both had to navigate through a trail of bodies. When he reached the vehicle, Taylor felt a large hand grasp his ankle. He looked down in horror to see a

Mech clinging to life and still trying to fight.

The creature tried to pull him off his feet, but a gunshot cracked behind him finished the creature for good. Taylor turned and nodded in gratitude to Jafar who had responded with lightning reactions, and he could see Grey was now out the trench and close behind them.

"This isn't safe," he stated.

"Relax, Captain."

"I'll relax when we're not standing in no man's land in full view of anyone who wants to blow our heads off."

"Where's that British resolve and confidence?"

"I'm confident in the defence of our trenches," he muttered.

Taylor ignored him and carried on to the twisted wreck of the vehicle. It was a medium tracked main battle tank he was plenty familiar with. Seeing the wicked damage on one of what used to be one of their own was a painful reminder of the battle for Brest when it had all begun. Ammunition had poured out through a gaping hole in the side, but the wet rack had stopped it from exploding. Smoke bellowed from the commander's hatch, and the driver's hatch was nowhere to be seen. It had most likely been blown clear.

The smell was acrid and as even more unpleasant than he had remembered it. A mix of burning metal with scorched electrical systems. All of that with the smell of burning grass where it still kindled. He stepped up to the tank, expecting to see the remains of a driver, but as he leapt atop the vehicle he stopped, surprised when he found the driver's compartment filled with electronics that were now all but destroyed.

"What is it?" asked Grey.

"That's why they came at us till the very end. There's no one driving 'em."

Grey looked confused and jumped up onto the hull to see for himself. Taylor could see he knew exactly what he was looking at, and it was starting to make sense.

"Remotely driven armoured fighting vehicles, not ever seen them in my life time," he stated. "They were banned by most nations over a century ago."

"Yeah, well I guess the rules went out the window some time back," he replied.

"Begs the question what else they'll be willing to throw at us?"

As he said it, a missile trail soared towards them.

"You spoke to soon!" yelled Taylor. They both leapt from the wreck, and the missile struck the turret. The explosion was near deafening as debris flew over them. Taylor looked back up to see specs in the sky closing in on them like a flock of birds. The ground rippled around them as automatic fire rained down on them.

"Cover!"

Taylor rushed to his feet and sprinted for the trench, gunfire erupting all around them. A bullet ricocheted off his shoulder armour and clipped his cheek and chin, cutting it badly as he rolled into the trench beside his comrades. They were already returning fire. He reached for his rifle, which was just where it had been left when he was tossed out of the trench, and slammed in a new magazine as quickly as could be managed.

As he took aim, he could see what was coming at them now, six rotor mini drone copters with an array of weaponry. They appeared to have little armour but were small and fast enough to be far from easy to hit. He squeezed the trigger, and the first shot went between two of the rotors and found no target. He followed it with a three-shot burst, and when one of the shots hit the hull of the drone, it dropped out of the sky. He lifted up his arms to protect himself as it dropped and smashed over his arms and helmet, along with several others that had been hit. As he got back up, he could see the body of a fallen man beside him. He grabbed the man's shield and took it as his own for cover.

He looked up from the shelter of the shield and could see dozens of drones circling them like vultures. Their trench provided no cover at all from the aerial attackers.

"We need to move!"

"No shit, Captain!" he replied. He looked up over the trench. The whole line was under attack in a similar fashion, and out in the distance a new wave of armoured vehicles was approaching.

"Fall back, back to the town!" he yelled down the comms.

He was the first out the trench with his shield held high as it took impacts. He looked back for just a second to be certain the rest of his unit were following suit. As he turned back to watch where he was going, one of the drones swooped in low so that it was level with his head. He lowered his shield and quickened his pace. A few light impacts glanced off his shield, but then he felt a larger one as he smashed into the drone, and it was thrown underfoot.

He kept up the pace to get further into the buildings of the town that were rather more intact than the outer areas they had left. He could see an old bank up ahead with thick walls and rushed for the door that was halfway off its sliding mechanism. A dozen or more of the Regiment rushed through with Silva last through the door. Parker was nowhere to be seen, but he had to hope she had made it to safety.

Taylor looked up, relieved to see the floor above were fortunately still solid. He turned back to peer through one of the windows and caught sight of several drones hot on the trail of some of his unit. One was holding his shield back to cover them the best he could, but shots were landing all around their position. Taylor rushed back to the half open door, took quick aim, and fired a burst at the cluster of drones.

One burst into flames and smashed down into the ground. The others banked sharply and came for him, but now they were right where he wanted them. They could only approach head on in the narrow corridor of attack he had left them. He held his shield firmly before him and his rifle at its side, using his helmet targeting to remain safe.

The shield absorbed a few shots while he blasted the drones out of the sky. As the last one fell, it launched another missile that smashed into the centre of his shield. The impact launched him into the building more than ten metres where he hit a support beam with his back and then crumpled to the ground. Mitch blacked out for just a few seconds as he landed and then turned to see Silva reaching for him. He coughed and spluttered; his lungs were filled with dust that had gathered on the floors of the abandoned bank.

His mouth was drier than ever now and coated in a thick layer of dirt and soot, making his voice coarse and husky. His head pounded, and he wanted nothing more than to rip his helmet off. He could feel his brain throbbing, and his skull dripping in sweat that now lined the helmet.

"You got a thing for acrobatics, Colonel. Should have joined the air force," said Silva.

"That's a big help," Taylor groaned.

Silva helped him to his feet, and he looked up. The half open doorway was now just a gaping hole and with no door of any kind in sight. A small fire had started beside it where the interior had ignited, and several of their unit were trying to put it out. It had quietened down outside now with only infrequent gunfire.

"Those things were banned under the Graz Convention a long time ago," he stated.

"Yeah, well I guess no one told the Germans."

"I still don't understand why they're fighting us, Sir," said Acosta.

Taylor barely knew the Private who had come over with Silva but had never seen combat with any of them, being too young to have fought in the last war.

"They are probably thinking just the same about us," replied Taylor.

"Yeah, well it ain't them getting invaded, is it?"

Taylor knew he had been an aggressor in their land before this had happened, but he couldn't bring himself to try and explain it to the young Private who was eager and loyal, but far from smart. Silva leaned in close to the Colonel.

"Why is it we always end up slap bang in the middle of the action, no matter where it might be?" he whispered.

Taylor smiled in response. "Because that's our purpose in life."

They heard a rustle of steps and raised their weapons in readiness, but were met by Sergeant Parker who rushed in through the doorway. Her face was cut in several places from debris, but she looked happy to have found them all.

"Well that's new," she gasped.

"Indeed, but I doubt it'll be the first surprise we see from the UEN," replied Taylor. "You heard from Dupont yet if we're getting the support we need?"

"Yes, Sir, that and more. Two divisions are deploying to the area presently. We are to redeploy to Meaux immediately."

"Meaux? Christ, that'll take us out of this war."

"I spoke to the General personally, Sir. Sounds like they've made some progress in regard to the Krys agents and want you there."

"And so they order the whole Regiment back?"

"Come on, Colonel," added Silva. "We're two hundred strong, might as well be your personal bodyguards. Hell you need it."

He looked around to see the news sat well with all who heard it.

"These two divisions, they're actually here?" he asked.

"Ten klicks out and with plenty of armour," replied Parker.

"And our ride out of here?"

"Already put down half a klick west and awaiting us."

"Then we wait till relieved. I ain't giving ground just to save a few minutes."

"The General was quite adamant that we were to redeploy immediately."

"Yeah, well he ain't here," replied Taylor dryly.

He tapped on his comms unit. "Everyone, stay put and keep a keen eye. And tell Captain Grey he's got time to brew up."

Several of the marines around him smiled.

"Acosta, gather up three of those drones as complete as you can find. I want to take 'em back for Reiter."

"He still working with us?" asked Silva.

"Bet your ass he is. We lost too many to these things, but it could have been a lot worse. I want to make sure next time we encounter them, they do not cause us so much trouble. Reiter will have a way."

"Hell, all you need is nets," said Acosta.

Taylor turned in surprise to hear the Private speak out and inject into their conversation. At first he took offence at it, but was then keen to hear what he had to say.

"Go on..."

"Those drones are hard for us to hit with a rifle round, Sir, but they ain't all that tough. Fire a net up, and you'll take them down easy."

"Where's this coming from?" asked Silva.

"When my daddy used to go fishing, he didn't harpoon each fish one at a time, he cast a net and made the job easy."

"Nets? Sure you don't mean your granddaddy?" jested Silva.

"He learnt with his pops and his before him, okay. He liked it that way."

"All right, all right," interrupted Taylor. "It's not a half bad idea. You can take it to Reiter when we get back."

"Me? No, Sir, I was just passing it on to you."

"You have a good idea, Private, then you better be prepared to act on it."

"Yes, Sir," he muttered nervously.

"We've got an armoured column coming up the road!" shouted one of the troops on guard outside.

Taylor lifted his comms. "Grey, cancel that brew. We're moving out!"

He took a little amusement in knowing just how the Captain's face would look at that moment before heading for the door. The first sight that struck him was that of five bodies of fallen comrades. They were loaded onto mechanical mules ready to move, and several others wounded beside them. Mitch wanted to tell them they were going home, but they no longer had one.

"To the boats, lets go!"

CHAPTER TWO

It was a short journey back to Meaux and an unexpected one at that. Ever since signing up with the European Alliance, they had been at the forefront of the conflict, which until recently had not erupted into total war. Many had been pondering over the frightening thought of nuclear powers facing off against each other once again. All knew from their schooling that such an event could be as potentially cataclysmic as the alien invasion they had lived through. But nobody would ask it openly, not until Acosta and his big mouth was sitting opposite the Colonel.

"Sir, why are we sitting by while we got nukes ready to use?"

Several others shook their heads but still listened in intently. They wanted answers as much as the inquisitive Private did.

"Because we're fighting a nuclear power, and using

them only assures mutual destruction."

"Not if we hit their silos first, go tactical on their asses."

"And their allies? Subs? Satellite silos?"

"Well, hell yeah, hit 'em all."

"You're a simple son of a bitch," Silva said.

"Several laughed, and it made him more than a little embarrassed, but he tried to brush it off.

"All been tried before," replied Taylor. "We start throwing nukes, and we can say goodbye to half the World's population. Hell we lost enough to the aliens."

"Yeah, but we're still fighting 'em!"

Taylor couldn't refute it. "You just leave the big decisions to others, Private. Those with the bigger picture and a greater understanding of these things."

"Like you do?" Parker asked.

Taylor smiled in response. He had gained a reputation for insubordination to the level it was now a joke amongst the Corps.

"Hey, when you reach Colonel, feel free to call the shots. Till that time, your ass is mine, and you'll do, think, and say whatever I want you to."

Several of the others laughed at him being put in his place, but all in good humour. They put down in the Meaux base shortly afterwards and found they were being welcomed by General Dupont himself with just a few of his personal staff. Taylor stepped down the ramp and sighed as he awaited the ribbing he was expecting, but to his surprise it never came.

"Welcome back, Colonel," said Dupont.

He was so polite Taylor wondered if he were even the same man he used to know. For just a few seconds, he considered the possibility the General himself was a Krys agent, but he let the thought settle to the back of his mind, realising it couldn't be true.

"You wanted us...me back for something big, what's the story?"

"You'll have to follow me. The rest of your unit can stand down. Canteen is open and awaiting them."

"I'd have a few join me, Sir."

"A handful of your most senior personnel."

He turned and pointed to Silva, Grey, and Parker.

"Better bring him along, too," Dupont said, pointing to Jafar.

They're finally learning to trust him, Taylor thought.

He turned to the others who hadn't bothered to fall in.

"Get some chow, and some sleep if I haven't found a job for you by the time you're done."

There were various grunts of relief and approval. Taylor joined the General as he got up to pace.

"So what's up?" he asked.

"When we get inside, Colonel."

They passed through into one of the administrative buildings that Taylor knew to house some of the research facilities. It was a vast six storey complex, with an array of anti-aircraft weapons fitted along its walls. It was the kind of stronghold many would choose to take shelter, and the last on Earth Taylor ever wanted to be because he knew what a target it made itself.

As they stepped inside, Taylor realised what a hive of activity it was; both researchers and military personnel rushed past them.

"Whatever you had to tell me can't be that much of a secret," said Taylor.

"Not a word leaves this building. Those operating here, live here presently. Until today, only three of my staff and myself have left this facility in the last month. Since you uncovered... and recovered the first Krys agent we have been working to determine what exactly they are."

"And hopefully in what numbers they are, and how we can identify the bastards."

"Yes, and many other questions which we are all asking."

"And have you found those answers?"

"Some of them."

They reached another level of security where three armed guards stopped them. They stood before a heavily reinforced blast door. It clearly had more than a single entry device.

"They're with me. Open the door," Dupont said casually.

The guards hesitated, looking suspiciously at the alien among the group, and then to Taylor who was still coated in dust and with a bloodied face. His rifle slung at his side was another cause for concern. One of the guards tried to talk, but the General interrupted him.

"Well don't just stand there, open the door!"

They jumped to action. Two of them pulled out key cards and held them before a scanner at each end of the door. A green light on a board of three lit up. Next the General stepped forward to a retina scanner, and it immediately flashed a second green light. Lastly, he typed in a passcode onto a small pad beside the retina scanner, and the last light went green. As the doors prised apart, they could see they were foot thick steel, and it was clear the entire section they were entering was proof against all but apocalyptic assault.

Castle within a castle, Taylor thought.

The room was filled with yet more busy personnel, and most of what they worked on went right over the Colonel's head. Dupont led them to a table where a few familiar faces sat, including Reiter. He nodded in a casual welcome and then turned his attention to a man he'd never expected to see again - Major Bryan Weller; his interrogator when he was incarcerated so long ago by Dupont and Schulz.

"What the hell part do you play in all of this?" he asked.

"There was a prisoner to interrogate," he replied dryly.

Taylor didn't hate the man. In fact, he had been remarkably civil during their time, but he still found it hard to forgive and work with him after all he had suffered during his time behind bars. That time cost him Friday's life, and that incident would forever be linked to Dupont and Weller for him.

"We seemed to have stepped past our difficulties for the greater good, Colonel. Can you not do the same?"

In danger of appearing as if he were throwing a tantrum, he righted himself and respectfully nodded. It was at least a relief they were working with him and not against him.

"All right, all this build up, let's hear what the fuck's going on."

"Colonel, we have assembled here the greatest minds at our disposal to try and answer all the questions we have had this past month and before. There is some chance of stopping this war, if we can prove to all parties that an alien force is pulling the strings here, but we need proof. Proof is the key. I will now hand you over to Marian Rossi, the lead researcher for this project."

Rossi looked to be no older than thirty-five, surprisingly young for the position of power and responsibility she was in. Her hair was tied up and out the way for her work, and thickly applied make up barely hid the weariness in her face; from what was clearly many sleepless nights of work. Despite that, she was strikingly attractive, a fact that did not go unnoticed to Parker as Taylor got lost in her eyes.

"So what are your findings?" asked Eli.

"Quite frankly they are not developed enough, but time is not on our side. I am here to tell you what we know so far. The specimen, K1, who you know as Councillor Armand, outwardly appears and is as human as you are. Internally, K1's organs are an exact to match ours, and dental records even match, assuming the original records were not tampered with."

"So we're no further ahead with it?" asked Taylor cynically.

"Be patient, Colonel," said Dupont.

Mitch grunted for the scientist to continue.

"I cannot say whether K1 is in fact a clone or not. Neither do we yet know whether K1 serves the Krys of his own volition. However, what I can tell you is he is not one hundred percent identical to humans."

Taylor's eyes lit up.

"The retinas are quite different and are lined with a technology we believe records all they see. Additionally, a microscopic transmitting device placed inside the brain is believed to transmit these images."

"Believe?"

"Colonel, you must understand, we are trying to understand technology which is perhaps hundreds of years more advanced than our own in so little time."

He nodded in agreement and appreciation for all she was doing.

"So if he's been transmitting all this time, they know

where he is, and what we're doing?"

Dupont interrupted.

"The K1 specimen was immediately quarantined upon arrival and placed within every form of barrier defence against transmission or detection we possibly have."

"As far as we know, the last images K1 could have transmitted were when he arrived here a month ago," Rossi added.

"That's a lot of maybes, Doc."

"I am sorry, Colonel, but we are doing all that we can."

"All right, so tell me more about this transmitter. Is it proof of alien tech and can it be easily identified?"

"Yes, it is not of Earth manufacture. An x-ray can identify this chip, assuming all Krys agents have them."

"And that's a big assumption," added Parker.

"We have to go with what we know, and what we have to work with," said Dupont.

"Anything else?" asked Taylor. "Anything else different about them? Are they stronger than us, see further? Hear better?"

Rossi shook her head. "They appear human in all other attributes."

"But you still can't tell if they're grown in a test tube or what?"

Dupont interrupted once again.

"Councillor Armand was a civil servant before the war, and like many who survived the war in Europe, we have little documentation showing where they were over the last few years. So yes, a man that looked like him existed; whether it is the same man, remains to be seen."

Taylor looked to his former interrogator who was waiting patiently.

"How far have you got with Armand?" Taylor asked him.

"About as far as I got with you."

"Then maybe you should consider a change of career."

"Silva could not help but laugh a little, but he tried to hide it.

"You must have got something out of him?" insisted Taylor.

Weller shook his head. "He's denying any knowledge of Krys agents and claims to be nothing more than his official title."

"Well, it's not like he's gonna give it up easily, is it?"

"My hands are tied, Colonel. There are hundreds of ways to interrogate a prisoner, but just as when I worked with you, our laws restrict me. There is little I can do but talk."

"Talk? You call talking interrogation? You're trying to find out secrets which could be vital to the survival of the human race."

Taylor turned to Dupont who shrugged in response.

"You're okay with this? Abide by every human rights law there is while this bastard sits pretty and gives us nothing?"

"And what would you have said if we broke those rules when you were behind bars?"

"I'd have fought you every step of the way, Weller, and I doubt you'd still be here today. But I don't give a goddamn what might, should, or could have been done. I care about this moment, right now."

"Need I remind you we have built our laws over thousands of years, and while they may not be perfect, it remains necessary to keep them intact to keep our humanity," said Rossi.

Taylor shook his head in disbelief.

"Great, Doctor, good for you. You hang on to those socialist ideals, and go and live in your fairy tale world where everything is just fucking amazing, and aliens don't come and try and fuck your shit up."

It silenced the room for a moment. Rossi's face turned to surprise and then disgust.

"You're a pig, Colonel," she replied defiantly.

"All right, enough!" Dupont shouted.

The room was silenced as he thought on the matter, and they looked to him for the way forward. He was looking down at the projection of Armand's brain still and almost in a daydream, thinking it over in his head until he finally looked up at them all.

"All I care about is ending this war in the shortest time possible, and with the fewest casualties on both sides.

Well, human casualties at least. Weller, whatever you are doing isn't working. It's time for a new approach."

"I must protest..." he began.

"Noted, but I'm not interested," replied Dupont.

The General turned to Jafar who had been standing back from the table behind Taylor and had remained silent throughout.

"Do you know anything at all about these Krys agents, or any cloning or reprogramming your people ever did?"

Jafar shook his head and simply replied, "Nothing."

"Well, you can still be useful. Right now, I'm organizing a meet with UEN representatives to try and get them to understand what is going on here, but it isn't going to be easy. We need all the evidence we can get."

"And what if the representatives we meet with are in fact more Krys agents?" asked Taylor.

"That's just a chance we'll have to take. I want info out of Armand, and you are going to get it, you and your alien friend here. You've got until whenever it takes me to organise this meet, probably a few hours, a day at most."

"And you are authorising me to do what, Sir?"

"Anything you have to. We need Armand alive. Besides that, use your own discretion."

"We cannot sink to this level of barbarism," protested Rossi.

"We do what we must. We all have much work ahead of us, and I will hear no more of your argument. I will not be swayed in this matter. Weller, you will show the Colonel to Armand's cell and provide him with any assistance he asks. Any more questions?"

"Yes, Sir," said Parker.

Taylor turned; surprised to hear her speak up.

"What is it, Sergeant? Speak your mind quickly."

"Sir, I only wonder, if Krys agents worked their way into the UEN, why not us as well? How do we know there aren't any of them among us, right now?"

"It is a fair question. This facility utilises an x-ray scanner for security measures at all entry points, initially intended to protect against hidden weapons and data devices being brought on site. Everyone in this room has been scanned and cleared."

"Based on evidence obtained from a single specimen," Reiter added.

It was the first words he had spoken since they had arrived, and it was met with a sigh from Dupont who had clearly been dealing with the scientist's cynical attitude throughout their work together. Before he could interrupt, Reiter continued.

"One specimen is not nearly enough to make the basis of any results. It does not even begin to scratch the surface."

Taylor looked to Rossi for her input.

"It is true. Other enemy agents may exhibit entirely different identifying features, or God forbid, none at all.

But until such time as we have further research subjects, we can only work with what we have."

Taylor couldn't help but feel that after everything they had done to secure Armand, he expected a lot more to have come of it.

"This bastard could be the key to ending the war. I'll be damned if we did all the hard work to get him, just to find it was all for nothing."

His comrades nodded and grunted in approval.

"Far from useless, Colonel," replied Rossi. "This has answered many questions for us, but in science, there is rarely an end to any research. It merely reaches one height and then strives for another."

"I'm glad you find it all so very interesting. It cost us lives to get that bastard, and it'll cost us many more if your work here doesn't end this war."

Rossi was silenced, and it was clearly more weight on her shoulders than she'd ever felt before.

"Enough talk, you all know what needs to be done. Get to it."

"As those around the table split away, Weller approached Taylor to be his guide and aid, but Mitch turned to Parker first.

"You get everyone of our Regiment through that scanner in the next two hours."

"You think some of them could be working for the enemy?"

"I don't want it to be true, but I want to know for certain. Every one of them, you understand?"

She nodded in agreement.

"Oh, and get Acosta to me ASAP."

She nodded in agreement and rushed off to go about her duties. Taylor eventually turned and acknowledged Weller's presence.

"Lead the way."

Weller led the three of them down a few corridors and through yet another security check with armed guards. They passed through the first barred door that was once again an unpleasant reminder of the time he had spent in such a prison. All he could think was to be grateful he was now a free man.

They passed through into a room where half the wall was glass and looked in on the Councillor. Clearly it was one-way glass, for he did not acknowledge their presence in any way. He sat upright on his bed with his back against the wall. Far from a man who had lost everything, he merely looked bored.

"You want the cameras turned off?" asked Weller.

Taylor shook his head.

"No, I'm not ashamed of what we have to do here, and I have the authority to do so."

"Doesn't mean you won't be breaking laws."

"I think we're a little past that. We get through another war, and we can worry about it then."

"That's always your attitude, isn't it, Colonel? Screw the rules now and worry about it later. No wonder you get yourself in so much shit."

"Yeah, and tend to get the job done right, too."

It was hard for Weller to argue with that.

Taylor looked to Grey as if to ask if he had any ideas, but the Captain merely responded with a question.

"You know anything about interrogation?"

"I figure I'll make it up as I go along, like half the shit we've had to do since all this began."

"Great plan," he mumbled.

Taylor turned to Weller. "So what have you tried so far?"

"I've tried to build a rapport with the subject, to become his friend, and offer incentives for his assistance,"

"And how'd that work?"

Weller shrugged his shoulders and said nothing.

"Right, so he didn't take the carrot. Time for the stick."

"That won't work, Colonel. Subjects will say the wildest of things under threat or use of physical pain. We need truths."

"A fighter might hold out until such time where they'll tell you anything, but he ain't a fighter. He's a big mouth in a suit. I doubt anybody's dared ever call him an offensive name, and you've merely carried on that routine. Look at him. He thinks he owns this place and owns you."

Taylor put his rifle down on the desk in front of him

and then paced over to the door leading to his cell. He wasn't surprised to see a smug smile on Armand's face when he entered the room. He had the look of a man who was untouchable. Taylor thought back to movies he had seen of wealthy criminals in the same position, who saw them as above the law and would rub it in at every opportunity.

I wonder if he has ever felt pain?

"Good to see you again, Colonel. I am glad to see you keeping well."

His voice was sleazy and insincere, to the point of being a little insulting.

"We both know you are a Krys agent, and soon the world will, too."

Armand shrugged. "And who cares anymore? The UEN and Mech soldiers stand together against you. The war has started now. Nobody cares for the reasons why, only of winning."

"You're wrong. And when we show the world your deceit, you will be done for."

"Then what are you doing here if not bore me to death?"

"You're gonna help me answer a few more questions."

"Because your plan of exposing Krys agents is going so well?"

Taylor reached for his Assegai quickly. He switched off the power so that it was nothing more than a truncheon.

To Armand's surprise, the Colonel leapt across the room and smashed the weapon into his face. The baton hit dead on his nose, and the impact was amplified as the wall he was resting against worked as a bump stop. Blood burst out from his nostrils and a deep cut in the centre.

The Councillor recoiled forward and squirmed in pain, cupping his nose and the blood dripped through his fingers. Taylor took a pace back, grabbed the only chair in the room, and took a seat before him as he continued to wince in pain.

"You think you're protected by our laws, but what you need to know is I have no care for them. I do what I think is right. That is my law, and in my law, you'd be dead. I will happily admit we need you, but we only need you alive. So, you can do this the easy way, and answer my questions to the best of your ability, or you can feel pain until you finally give up and tell me anyway. So what'll it be?"

"Fuck you!" he yelled, blood spewing out from his mouth and over the floor.

Taylor lifted his baton and smashed it down on Armand's right kneecap. The sound it made on impact was stomach churning and made Armand scream at the top of his voice. Taylor took no pleasure in it, and the only thought in his head was that he was glad Parker was not in the room and watching him.

"At some point you will come to realise that I will stop at nothing to protect this world from those who wish to destroy it. The day your people understand that will either be the day they stop trying, or the day there is no longer any of you left to fight."

Armand sat back against the wall again, still in a lot of pain, breathing hard, and not daring to speak another word he knew would lead to more pain.

"So, I'm gonna ask you some questions, and you are going to answer them to the best of your knowledge. If you are lying, or telling half-truths, or if I even think you are bullshitting me, you know I will not hesitate to make you suffer for it. Death would be painless, but that is not what you'll get. At least not anytime soon."

He waited for an answer, but none came. He took it as a sign of acceptance.

"How many Krys agents are operating on Earth?"

He shook his head.

"I really don't know."

"So you may not know totals, I get it. But what sort of ballpark figure are we talking, a few dozen, few hundred, thousands?"

His eyes lit up at the last word.

"Thousands? How many thousands?"

"I don't know for certain, but enough are infiltrated in every level of your society that is needed to fuel this war."

"And what do you think will happen when we show UEN leaders this video of you confessing it?"

"Nothing. It's too late for you, Colonel. Years too late

for you to stop this."

He knew he wasn't getting anywhere, so he moved on.

"We found a chip in your head and some modifications to your retinas, are these features shared with all Krys agents?"

"I don't know."

Taylor lifted his Assegai over the man's other kneecap, but he quickly screamed out.

"I really don't know!"

Taylor relaxed.

"Do you know every item of your anatomy?" asked Armand.

Taylor knew he could be lying, but he also knew any answer on the subject could be wrong, whether he believed he was telling the truth or not.

The door to the cell suddenly prised open, and both turned sharply to see why. Weller stepped through into the room, and Armand relaxed back in relief.

"What is it?" asked Taylor.

"It's sterling work, Colonel," he replied. "If a little blood was all it took, you may well be able to rewrite the textbooks yet, just don't expect to win any peace prizes."

"Peace prize? Hell the only peace prize I want is the head of the last alien who would dare step foot on this planet."

"I can take it from here, Colonel," he replied.

"Now that I've done the hard work?"

"Now that you've done what I'm not allowed to. Now please leave us, Colonel. I have a whole host of questions I need answers to."

Taylor was actually relieved to be able to end it there. It wasn't work he liked at all. He got up and stepped up closer to Armand, who cringed at the sight of the marine looming over him with the baton that had dealt him so much pain.

"I'm heading out, but I won't be far away. I ain't going anywhere. You will answer all of Weller's questions no matter what, or I will return, and you don't want me to have to come back. Got it?"

He nodded in agreement, still sheltering his head and expecting to be struck. But Taylor would not. He didn't hurt the man for fun and through sadistic nature. He sheathed the Assegai and walked out of the cell.

"He gave in easy," said Grey.

"Yeah, either he really is as weak as he looks, or he knows the info he has will do us no good anymore."

"We can hope."

Taylor grunted as they stepped out from the room to find Parker and Acosta waiting for him.

"Get what you wanted?" Eli asked him.

"I think I got through, but God knows if anything we get from him will be of any use."

"So what now?"

"Follow me, Acosta with me."

The young Private looked fearful as he stepped up beside the Colonel and they got up to speed.

"That idea you had for taking down drones, it's time to share it with someone who can make it a reality."

"But...Sir...it was just an idea..."

"Every piece of tech we got sprung from an idea. I'm not asking you to design and build it, just share your concept, and we'll see what we can get done."

"But it might not work, Sir. It might be a piece of shit... sorry, Sir, junk, piece of junk."

"Yeah, well you let the experts be the judge of that. We were lucky we didn't lose a lot more last time we faced those things. In open ground or supressed by armour and artillery, they could have made mincemeat of us. We cannot afford, and I will not accept those losses. You came up with something that might save lives. Let's see where it goes."

The Private looked shocked and scared at the idea as he was led back to the research room where they'd had their briefing. He was taken to Reiter, who was busy working on a piece of electronics which none of them understood or recognised. As they approached, he turned and smiled.

"Good to see you are still alive," he said to Taylor, looking at the battle damage of his armour.

"Thanks in no small part to your equipment."

"What can I do for you?"

"The UEN attacked us with drones. They came as a

swarm with mostly short-range weaponry. They're light, fast, and agile, but lack any kind of protection. We need a simple way to knock them out of the sky, and this young marine here thinks he has a solution. I'll leave him with you and see how you do."

Acosta's pulse seemed to stop, and he looked even more fearfully at Taylor.

"Sir..."

"You've got nothing to worry about. We improvise and overcome. It is what I expect of every man and woman under my command. You're the kind of new blood I need, and this is the kind initiative I want to see more of. Good luck with it."

He turned and left, leaving the Private speechless.

"Poor lad, he'll never have a clever idea again," said Grey.

Taylor laughed.

"So we have this evidence of a Krys agent and his recorded testimony, now what?"

"Dupont is arranging his meeting with UEN representatives. We just have to hope they're willing to listen."

"And what about the thousands of agents that may be out there?"

Taylor sighed at the very thought.

"I guess we just have to hope he's exaggerating."

But deep down he knew it was almost certainly true.

He'd seen the incubation chambers himself, and he'd heard Tsengal's report of the vast quantities Chandra had stumbled upon.

"However many there may be among us, there are still plenty of good people involved in this; every bastard who fought and survived the last war for a start. We just have to get through to them."

"So what now?"

"I haven't sat in a comfortable chair in weeks, and I intend to find one. Followed by something to eat and a few hours of sleep wouldn't go amiss. Whatever happens with this Armand situation, you can be guaranteed we'll be needed before long."

"Always us, isn't it?" asked Parker from behind them.

"Yep," he replied. "That's why we were put on this earth."

They got to the door they had entered the facility from, and Taylor took note of the subtle x-ray frame of the corridor just as Dupont had said.

"Hell of an idea that. If any Krys human can be identified that way, we may have hope yet."

At the doorway was a line of troops from the base being ushered in through the scanners one at a time, and clearly oblivious as to the reason why. They were being led into briefing rooms, most likely the explanation they were given as to being there.

Taylor stepped out into the warm light of day and saw

a sight he could not have expected, but always hoped for. Captain Charlie Jones stood before them in fatigues and armour, ready to go.

"Well, well. I guess the farm life isn't for you, after all, Charlie."

"Got that right," he replied.

"You back for good? Back to join the Inter-Allied Regiment. The rogues who are AWOL from their prospective home countries?"

He nodded in agreement. Taylor couldn't believe he had made it. After their last meeting, he never imagined the Captain returning to service and leaving his new life behind.

"Damn good to have you back!"

CHAPTER THREE

"Cheers!" called Grey.

They lifted their glasses high and then threw back the French cider. It was, course, acidic compared to anything Taylor had been used to getting back home, but it went down smoothly after the long day they had all experienced. Taylor was surprised Jones had not done the honours, but he was a different man to the one Taylor had once stood beside in battle. He couldn't blame Charlie for feeling the way he did, now that they were once more serving so close to where he had once been imprisoned by the invaders.

Taylor looked over to Eli, and a beaming smile stretched across her face.

Is this what it takes? A new war to brings friends back together to enjoy themselves?

Taylor was starting to wonder if he was born for war, as he seemed to be incapable of wanting any other venture.

He was deep in thought and reflection when Eli began calling him, and she had to yell his name a few times over the chatter. Finally, he turned to look at her, and she was curious as to where his mind was. She leapt out of her chair and rushed over to sprawl out over his lap, spilling a little cider over his as she did.

"First night in a while we can enjoy ourselves, and you look so serious. What's up, Colonel?" she asked casually.

"Nothing that you don't already know. I am merely taking in all that is before us. It is great, is it not? Having everyone back together?"

"I never thought you so sentimental?"

Taylor shook his head.

"No, you never appreciate what you have until its gone, do you?"

She only smiled in response.

Within thirty minutes, the two were falling into bed after just a few drinks, all that they could allow themselves while danger remained so close. Exhaustion overcame them, and they were asleep within minutes.

Taylor arose with the sunrise to find Eli was still in a deep sleep. It amused him to watch her for a few moments before reaching for his uniform. It was the best rest he had gotten in weeks and stepped out of his quarters to feel the fresh morning air on his face. The war hadn't reached Meaux. At times it was easy to forget they were once more in a state of war. Mitch began to pace through the base, for no other reason other than to take a stroll.

But after a few blocks, a sight that was a grim reminder of their current situation, the base hospital, hit him. Engineers were busy fabricating temporary structures beside it to quell the overcrowding that had already begun. He stood and watched two light armoured vehicles roll up to the hospital. They were battle scarred, and Taylor quickly took interest, recognising the unit markings as those belonging to Dubois' unit.

He'd no idea if she had returned to service or not, but a feeling in his stomach made him fear it so. The crew of the vehicles leapt out and pulled the wounded out from the rear doors. One of the casualties had the slender female figure that matched her description.

He rushed forward to check, but he already knew it would be her. As he approached, her face came into view, but she was not moving. He didn't want it to be her, despite already knowing it was. Somehow, he hoped he could wish it away, but as he stepped over, her face was unmistakeable. He looked up to the crew and the medic who were carrying her.

"How is she? She gonna make it?"

"They all seemed to recognise the Colonel, but he didn't remember meeting them. The medic shook his head.

"We can hope. She's taken a lot of shrapnel and is in a bad way."

She writhed a little, and Taylor finally noticed she was

at least still breathing. She looked up for just a moment to see and recognise Taylor, trying to reach for his arm before passing out.

"Do not let her die!" he yelled.

They rushed on into the hospital, and he shook his head in disbelief. He lifted up his comms unit.

"Jones, I need you ASAP."

No response came.

"Somebody find me Captain Jones, and contact me ASAP!"

He looked around and suddenly felt helpless. His old friend had finally returned to them, and he knew this could well break him. "Shit," he said to himself, sitting down on a small wall outside the hospital. He had no idea what to do with himself. He waited for ten minutes and had still not received contact from any of his unit. He was getting frustrated and lifted his comms unit.

"Where the hell is Jones? Somebody speak to me."

Grey finally responded.

"No sign of the Captain, Sir."

Taylor shook his head.

"Well where the hell is he? Keep looking and get him to the hospital quickly. He needs to be here!"

He rushed into the hospital to find Dubois. One of her comrades guided him into her room where he could look in. It reminded him of the time he'd stood watching over Parker when she had been wounded early on in the first war, and he remembered how tough Dubois was.

A doctor stepped out from the room to address him and two of her comrades who stood beside Taylor.

"She will need some surgery, but she is stable. You can have a few minutes with her, but please keep her calm."

"Thank you," he replied, stepping into the room.

Dubois was weak and barely able to turn her head and speak.

"You're a sucker for punishment," he said. "Every time a war starts, you go headlong into it and almost get yourself killed."

"That's rich," she whispered, "coming from you."

It brought a cautious smile to his face.

"You'll have Charlie sick, if we can ever find him."

She nodded a little in agreement.

"He's here one minute and gone the next. Always was the same."

She looked confused.

"Here? When?"

"He got here yesterday afternoon. He's signed back up with us. Best thing that's happened since all this kicked off."

She shook her head.

"No, no," she said.

Taylor was confused by her comment and tone.

"What is it?"

"He is not here. He would not go and fight again."

"Maybe he changed his mind."

She shook her head, coughing and trying to get her breath.

"I spoke to him last night. He was at home on the farm. He begged me to return."

"Hate to tell you, but he was here drinking with us."

She shook her head once again.

"No, on video, he was at the farm."

Taylor almost stopped breathing, beginning to piece together what she was saying. Jones arrived out of the blue and was the only one in the Regiment who hadn't been cleared by the x-ray scanners.

Taylor opened his mouth to speak but was interrupted by an alarm sounding throughout the base.

"What is it?" asked Dubois.

Taylor turned to her two comrades. You stay here and look after her. If you see Captain Jones, you approach with caution and arrest him immediately, you hear?"

They didn't understand, but they did accept the command. Taylor rushed out of the room as quickly as he could and burst out of the hospital and across the two blocks to the research bunker where the alarm had originated. Two guards were rushing for the door, and he quickly followed them. He had no weapons or armour on him. It took a minute for the guards to get through the security door.

As they entered, one ran through a pool of blood

emanating from a soldier who lay dead with her throat cut. Taylor stepped over and knelt down to take a closer look. As he did, he spotted another body with a blade embedded in the eye socket.

"What the hell happened here?" asked one of the soldiers.

"We have a traitor among us, an enemy agent. Get to the research labs, and secure Rossi and her staff. I'm heading for the cells."

"Why?"

"Just trust me."

Taylor stepped over to the other body and was glad to find a pistol still holstered. He grabbed it and the two spare magazines on the fallen soldier's belt before carrying on down the corridor. Civilian staff members were running past in fear and pointing the way he was going to tell him where the attacker was.

How quickly things can go to shit, he thought to himself.

He carried on with nothing more than the sidearm he had recovered. When he arrived at the cellblock, he found another dead guard and a trail of blood going through the open doorway to the cells. The fallen guard had been shot this time, in what was clearly becoming a hastier situation.

Taylor's instincts had quickly cut in, but he was still rolling it all over in his head and trying to make certain he was right about the scenario. He stepped through the doorway, hoping to find nothing but knowing he would.

He knew all but one of the cells were empty, so he headed directly for Armand, but as he turned the bend to get to the cell door, he found Jones helping the former Councillor to escape.

Armand had to hop and be dragged because the damage to his kneecap was substantial. It meant they were making little progress.

"Stop!" Taylor ordered.

He had the pistol raised high and could see Jones was armed just the same; BDUs and a pistol he'd picked up from a body. Jones snapped around and fired two shots. The first went wide, but the second would have met its target had Taylor not leapt back behind the corner where he'd come from. Mitch took in a deep breath, realising how naked he felt without his armour. It had saved his life more times than he could count, and now a single shot could end his life.

"I know who you are, Jones!" Taylor shouted.

It seemed strange to call him that, but he couldn't think of what else to say. This seemed like all the evidence needed to know this Jones was a Krys agent, but he still wanted to hear it from his lips to know for sure.

"Then why didn't you shoot me?"

"To give you a chance to surrender. Lay down your weapon and give yourself up!"

"Why, so I can be a lab rat like Armand here?"

"That or I put a bullet between your eyes."

He went silent for a moment and thought about it.

"You couldn't kill me, your oldest living friend."

"But you're aren't him, you just look like him."

"You've lost this war, Colonel Mitch Taylor. You've won a few battles, but you could never win the war. This planet is infiltrated beyond your understanding, and it'll fall around you in a flash."

"Yeah, well, we'll see about that. I can't let you take Armand, and he isn't fit enough to run, so what'll it be?"

There was silence for an uncomfortable ten seconds where all Taylor could hear was the alarm still ringing in his ears. He dared not sneak a peek around the corner. He knew how good a shot Jones was. Finally Jones replied.

"If I can't have Armand, neither can you."

As he said it, a small explosion erupted nearby from beyond Jones' position. It was too coincidental to not be Jones who was the cause. He cautiously looked around the corner, and Jones was gone. A man-sized hole had been punched in a wall at the end of the corridor, and Armand's body lay lifelessly between him and the breach.

At first he couldn't understand why Jones had left his fellow Krys agent behind, but as he closed the distance, he understood. Blood spewed out over the floor where Armand had been decapitated. His head was gone; containing the only evidence they had uncovered which identified Krys agents.

"Shit!"

He rushed to the breach in the wall and passed through without any care for his own life. He knew that evidence was more important than anything on the entire base. A trail of blood spots continued on up another corridor that he quickly followed. Two gunshots rang out in the distance, and he already knew that would be another friendly down.

What is this shit? Friends are enemy agents. This could end us.

He carried on and found the body of one of the French guards, just as he suspected. The man was still breathing but couldn't move.

"Where does this lead to?" asked Taylor impatiently. "Where is he heading?"

The soldier could barely breathe or speak, but just about summed up enough energy to point onwards and mumble the word 'hangar'.

Fuck, he's gonna try and fly out of here.

He knew the chances of him making it across the border were slim, but if they were shot down en route, all evidence of them would be destroyed anyway. Taylor knew if they got airborne it was a 'win win' for the Krys. He picked up the pace and stormed down the corridor, without a care for anything in the world except for stopping Jones. He knew at any moment he could be ambushed but took no caution at all. He could not afford to.

The corridor opened up ahead of him as the Frenchman had said. He burst out into a small hangar that stored just three small craft; highly agile and fast hexrotor transports with power turbines derived from alien technology. They seated half a dozen at the most, and Taylor realised they must have been there for rapid evac of VIPs. A fact that might get them over the border, free and clear.

The engines were already fired up and the massive blast doors in front of them sliding apart. Taylor had just twenty seconds before he'd lose them for good. He looked to the cockpit and could see Jones looking down at him with a triumphant smile. It was bizarre and incongruous to be coming from a man he'd considered his closest friend for so many years. He had to keep telling himself that it was not Jones.

Taylor raised his pistol and fired two shots at the glass, but both bounced off with no damage. He quickly turned his attention to one of the turbine engines and fired two shots through, but they ricocheted off as well. He looked around for anything that could make a difference and saw the mechanics tool rack. He grabbed the largest wrench he could and launched it into the turbine. It crunched and bounced around inside the engine before being tossed out the back to little effect.

He looked out to see the doors were almost open. There were just a few seconds left. Then to his side he noticed huge chains hanging from a hoist, presumably designed for lifting large component parts. He grabbed one of the chains and rushed to the craft. The hoist swung over on its mountings overhead, and as Jones upped the power to move, Taylor launched the chain into the turbine. As it struck the fan, a huge piece of metal flew from the engine and narrowly missed Taylor's head. He recoiled back and fell to the floor.

He watched in amazement as the thick chain was pulled through the engine until it went taut and ripped the hoist from the ceiling. The huge electronic pulley system crashed down onto the turbine, crushing it in one and ripping part of the fuselage off the craft as it did so.

The turbine caught fire for a moment. The aircraft's emergency systems cut in, and all power was reduced, and the fires put out by its inbuilt extinguishers. The noise finally died down, and Taylor could see the craft was beached and utterly useless. Jones still glared at him from the cockpit. He had no choice now but to confront Taylor personally.

"Only way out is through me, you son of a bitch!" yelled Taylor.

He got to his feet and took cover behind a mechanic's workstation and slammed a new magazine into his pistol. A few seconds later, the door to the craft slid open, but there was no sign of Jones. Then a gunshot rang out, and Taylor ducked down as it hit the top beside him. It hadn't come from the door of the craft. He looked out around the corner and saw as another gunshot rang out that it was coming from the hole that had been ripped in the fuselage.

Taylor took a few paces along to change position and

then jumped up to fire a few shots, but he could not tell if they met their target. Three shots were returned at him, and he ducked down once again. In this instance, time was on his side. Any time now he hoped for a swathe of soldiers to rush to his aid, and yet they hadn't come yet.

Two more shots rang out, and then all went quiet. Taylor waited for a moment before carefully looking over the edge to see Jones' silhouette in the doorway of the craft. He stood square on with no care for cover and his pistol lowered.

"I'm out!" he called.

"Tough shit!"

"You won't shoot me, Mitch. You couldn't shoot an old friend!"

"No, I couldn't, but you're not him! Jones never came back to service. Your secret is out!"

"Ah, well, can't win 'em all."

Taylor found it unnerving how much this Krys agent sounded and acted like Jones. He watched from cover as Jones threw his pistol away onto the ground and stepped out onto the deck of the landing area. Mitch rushed out with his pistol held at the ready. He could see Jones carried the head of Armand in one hand and a bloodied knife was stuffed into his belt.

"Maybe you won't kill me for looking like him, but you will not kill me because I'm the only living clone you know."

Taylor couldn't help but agree.

"So I'm going walk to that next ship and fly the hell out of here."

He turned to leave, but Taylor fired a warning shot at the floor beside him that forced him to stop.

"You're not going anywhere. I need you alive, but you don't need your legs. Another step towards that craft, and I'll put you down."

"You put animals down. You want to put me down, you better be willing to do it with your own hands."

He dropped the head of Armand and drew his knife, but he did not grip it ready to fight. Instead, he threw it away.

"You going to shoot an unarmed man?"

The clone standing before him disgusted Taylor. It was an insult to his friend, and an insult to their Regiment, and yet he could not help but treat it like a human.

"All right, you want to do this?" he asked. "You're coming with me, whether you like it or not."

He dropped the magazine on his pistol and placed it down on the workbench. He didn't enjoy hurting Armand because the Councillor either didn't or couldn't fight back, but he was going to enjoy this.

"You know you Krys play every card against the human race, and every time we beat you. You just don't know when to quit."

"When we own this planet, this heaven, and we will

own it. No matter the cost, no matter how long it takes. Erdogan is coming for you, and nothing will stand in his way."

"Wrong, I will."

He rushed forward at Jones and tackled him to the ground, beating down on him with two heavy punches to the face. Jones tried to cover his face, but Taylor worked a heavy shot to his flank, but as he did Jones managed to lever out from under him and lock a leg over his neck, launching him off onto his back. Jones kicked towards his head, but Taylor rolled over and was quickly back on his feet.

One-on-one combat was something he'd become intimately familiar with since he had been used as a gladiator in the ring. He rarely enjoyed that experience, but this was different. Now he had a reason to fight. Taylor stepped forward with his hands held at the ready and launched a fast jab towards Jones, who blocked and kicked to the inside of his leg. It hurt like hell and forced him to wobble, but he just about managed to stay on his feet when a kick hit his stomach and launched him back against the workbench where he had placed the gun. For a moment, the thought of reaching it passed through his mind, but his honour stopped him.

"It's a wonder you ever commanded this unit when Jones was clearly the better man," said the clone.

"Maybe he was, but you're not him."

Taylor rushed forward with immense speed and threw a jab as he done before, but stopped short in a feint that got the same response as before. Jones leapt aside. As he did, Taylor carried through with a hook, catching Jones square on the chin. He dropped to the floor. Taylor circled him with a smile. The clone held onto its jaw that had almost been broken by the impact.

"Jones was many things, great at many things in fact, but he was never one for a fist fight, and if you have nothing more in the bank than he had, you might as well give up now."

It still struck Taylor as strange to be hitting the man he considered such a strong friend. He had to keep reminding himself that it was not Jones, and that was easy when he was being attacked, but looking down at the body of Jones on the floor made him feel awkward and made it difficult to hit him while he was down.

"Might as well give up. You're not getting out of here."

"You are all that stands between me and that ship," he spat back.

"Like I said, might as well give up now."

Jones got back to his feet and stumbled towards Taylor as if half finished. Taylor lowered his guard, and as he did, Jones kicked once again to the leg that had been struck before. This time it buckled. A knee coming for his face quickly followed it. Taylor tried to lift his hands to protect his head, but most of the impact hit him full on and launched him onto his back.

The clone rushed past to make it to the ship, but Taylor took a firm hold on his ankle and pulled him off his feet. He landed hard but reached for the wrench that had blasted out the turbine a few minutes before and smashed it down on Taylor's arm. Mitch felt the bone crunch as it came close to breaking and hurt like hell. He could not help but release his grip and roll out the way as the wrench came at him once again, and smashing into the metal floor where he had lain.

Taylor's arm almost gave way when he pushed himself up. He knew another blow like that could stop him in his tracks. He reached for the first thing to hand, a two-metre metal tube. He had no idea what it was from, but it was lightweight for its size and completely rigid and tough. He held out the pole in both hands as if it were a spear, offering the tip to Jones to try and reach for it.

Jones struck towards the pole with his heavy wrench, but Taylor quickly avoided it, using the leverage of the light weapon and thrust it into his attacker's chest. The impact hit hard with no flex at all, and the wind was taken out of the clone's lungs. Taylor took his opportunity to finish it. He swung the pole around, striking Jones' leg and taking it out from under him. But Taylor did not stop the swing of the pole. He used the weight to pendulum it around his head and drive it into Jones' face.

The impact hit his skull just above his eye sockets and

instantly knocked him unconscious. Taylor took a deep breath and sighed in relief. He knew how close they had come to losing all the evidence they had. He stepped over to the head of Armand and picked it up off the ground as he heard footsteps thundering down the corridor towards him.

Four French soldiers rushed out into the hangar with rifles held high, and General Dupont himself with gun in hand followed them. They all stopped and looked in disbelief at the sight before them. Taylor stood with the pole in one hand and the severed head in the other; the hangar itself looked like a warzone. Dupont looked out at the open hangar doors and back to Taylor, trying to make sense of what had happened.

"Is that Armand's head you are carrying?" he asked.

Taylor nodded and couldn't help but admit it must be a bizarre sight to behold, but it was clear the General already knew Jones was the infiltrator.

"Captain Jones, one of yours from the very beginning."

"Near enough," replied Taylor, "but that isn't him. That is a Krys agent."

"We know. He was detected passing out scanners as he entered this building, but he cut a bloody path through."

"Something tells me it's time you upgraded your security. The clone got through to Armand and tried to bust him out. When I stopped him from doing it, he took the head for obvious reasons and made a break for it."

"So now we have no surviving Krys subject?"

"We have him. He'll live."

"Is the real Captain Jones still alive also?"

Taylor nodded in agreement, and Dupont's face lit up.

"This is a real boost to our position. If we can get the real Jones and clone together, it will be irrefutable proof of what the Krys have been doing."

"Yeah, well good luck getting him here. He doesn't want anything more to do with this war."

"Like it or not, he's in it; more than ever now."

"Well you can be the one to tell him that."

"Something tells me he'll be more amenable to the idea now. He's got a clone running around raising hell and a wife in the hospital. Wouldn't that drive you to want to fight back?"

"It would, yes," he replied. Though he didn't agree it would for Jones. The last time he saw the real Jones he was not the man he used to know, not even close. He wanted nothing more than to have him back alongside in the Inter-Allied Regiment. He looked down at the body of the clone and thought not of his own pain and the casualties they had suffered that day, but for the hatred he had for the clone making him believe he had his comrade back.

Dupont looked around again at the devastation all around Taylor.

"Do you destroy everything where you go?"

Taylor smiled in response.

"I never look for these fights. They just seem to land in my hands, or some wise ass throws me in the shit."

"It's good work here. We came so close to losing our evidence. Voice recordings, video footage, documented evidence; they are all pointless without the specimen as proof. We could have lost that, and now we have furthered our inventory."

"Where do we go from here?"

"I've got a meet arranged with UEN representatives, and you're just the man I need for it."

"Not going yourself, Sir?"

He shook his head. "Can't risk it, and anyway, your name means a lot to many people. If anyone can get the point across, it's you."

"I'm no ambassador or negotiator. I'm a marine, a fighter. You want to send a fighter to try and negotiate for peace? Only way I know how to win peace is to kill the enemy."

"You'll do just fine."

Well that's fucking great, he thought.

"Get to the hospital and have them make sure you're all okay, and go see Jones' wife while you're at it. I want you and your senior officers for a briefing at 1300 hours."

He dropped the pole, threw the head over so that it rolled to a halt beside the clone's body, and strode on out, leaving the soldiers in amazement at what they had seen. As he headed towards the hospital, he realised just how much he ached from the fight. The wrench strike to the arm had hit the bone in his forearm, and it was now swelling and a little numb.

Sometimes he felt as if he and his unit did everything in the war, and then he arrived at the hospital and was reminded how small a part they played in the overall picture. Parker was waiting for him at the door.

"What the fuck's going on?" she asked.

"You know Jones came back to us yesterday?"

"Yeah."

"It wasn't Jones."

"Shit."

"No kidding."

They walked on into the hospital to find Dubois, but they found an empty room. Mitch grabbed a nurse walking by.

"Sergeant Dubois, she was in this room, where is she now?"

"In surgery, Sir," he replied.

"Dubois? What's she doing here?" asked Eli.

Taylor couldn't bring himself to explain it, and he'd had enough of the stuffy air inside the hospital. It was air conditioned, but like all hospitals, it never smelt or felt good. He stepped outside and sat at a bench beneath a shelter extending over the front of the building, resting his head back against the wall. The sun was up now and it was baking hot; his exhaustion made him fall asleep where he sat.

It was an hour later when he awoke and found Parker still sitting beside him. A shadow passed over him, and he saw the silhouette of a man in front of him. He cupped his hand over his eyes to see it was Jones, though he barely recognised him. He wore casual civilian trousers and a loose khaki shirt. He had a beard now, longer hair, and looked nothing like the strictly disciplined Captain Jones he had known so well. It was at this point he thought if he had been in contact with his old friend, he would have known the clone to be false.

"Is it really you?" asked Taylor.

"I should have known you'd be at the centre of all this," replied Jones.

Taylor got up off his feet and offered out his hand in friendship, but Jones would not take it.

"Of course it's me, who else would I be?" he responded bluntly.

"Trust me, we've got a lot to discuss."

"I didn't come here to join you. I didn't come to fight. I came here for my wife."

Taylor was surprised to hear it. He thought Charlie might have finally come around, and it was a great disappointment to hear it was not the case.

"She out of surgery yet?" he asked.

Taylor shrugged and looked to Eli who didn't have an answer either.

"I'd like to know as much as you do."

"Did you speak to her when she arrived?"

Taylor nodded. "I told her you'd come back to us, and you had. That's what we need to talk to you about. Captain Charlie Jones drank with us last night, and this morning cut a bloody path through this base. It was because of Dubois I discovered he was not you, but too late to save as many lives as I would have liked."

Jones didn't seem to care for any of what he was saying.

"I want to see her," he responded.

Taylor led him inside to the room where he had first seen Dubois and was glad to see she had returned. They stepped through into her room, and she smiled on seeing Jones approach.

He looked over to the nurse tending her.

"How is she?"

"Well, she should make a full recovery in a few months."

A tear dropped down his cheek as he took her hand.

"I almost lost you."

"But you didn't," she replied.

Dubois was drowsy and barely able to stay awake.

"She needs plenty of rest," said the nurse.

Dubois beckoned for Jones to come a little closer, so he knelt in, but they could all just about hear Dubois' faint voice.

"I want you to do something for me," she said.

"What? Anything," he replied.

"Fight, fight for us."

He stood upright and looked into her eyes to see her sincerity and knew what he must do. It was a moment of clarity he'd not known in a long time. He turned to Taylor who could see new life in his old friend's face.

"These bastards mean to take everything from me, and I don't intend to let them without a fight. I want my commission back," he snapped.

"You have it."

* * *

Inter-Allied was formed up and anxiously waiting to hear what was coming next.

"All gather in!" Taylor ordered.

They were a little shocked at his relaxed approach and ambled forwards.

"Come on!" he yelled.

"We have a new mission on our hands, but not for the Regiment; for just six of us. No mission we have ever undertaken has been safe or with any certainty of returning, and this is far from an exception to the rule. Six of us are going to a meet with the enemy where we frankly have no idea what to expect, or if they'll keep they word of a ceasefire. I am gonna ask for volunteers."

"I'll go with you," Jones added quickly.

Taylor knew it wasn't a good idea throwing him into a

situation so soon after returning to service and with the stress of his wife's hospitalisation, but he could not say no to an old friend. He nodded in appreciation.

"I'll go," stated Grey.

Taylor shook his head.

"I'd be glad to have you at my side, but should this mission fail, and we not return, the Regiment will need experienced officers to move forward."

CHAPTER FOUR

Taylor waited outside his quarters for Jones who was making use of his room. The door finally opened, and Jones stepped out like a new man, standing tall and proud like he used to. He was clean-shaven and his hair shaved at the back and sides.

How sad that all he needed to recover was the near death of his wife. Although it was as much what she said as what has befallen her.

"We have a lot of work ahead of us, do we not?" asked Jones.

"More than you can imagine and then some," replied Taylor.

"Then I am in this till the very end with you. Whatever it takes for my Dubois to lead a life of peace. I will hunt all those who wish to destroy us to the end of the galaxy, should it be required."

Taylor smiled. He appreciated the sentiment, but he tried to lighten the tone.

"Dubois? You're married, and yet still call her by her family name?"

"It is how I first knew her. Her name is Coco, Coco Dubois, and that is how I will always know her."

"Sounds like it's working out for you, unlike your first marriage."

Jones smiled, the first time Taylor had seen him smile in years.

"Don't remind me."

For the first time in a long time, he saw hope that his closest band of friends were returning to what they were, unstoppable. He only wished they hadn't lost so many along the way.

"You know what you are fighting for now? What drives you now? It's what has fuelled the fire inside me all these years. You think I don't want to settle down to a quiet life with a beautiful woman, too?"

"No," Jones replied quickly.

Taylor was surprised by his brisk retort.

"I think you enjoy this. Never have you been more content than when you had an enemy to fight. You thrive on it, and it is why you lead us. You are the purest fighter among us. Unwavering, unflinching. You are the perfect soldier."

Taylor didn't know whether to take it as a compliment

or an insult, for it could be both in equal measure.

"Except I'm no soldier, I'm a marine."

"You used to be. What are you now as an officer in the European Alliance Army?"

Taylor didn't have a response. His Marine heritage had been drummed into him his entire life, as he had done to all under his command. He doubted the feeling would ever leave him, but it was food for thought. He was born into a world where he had the weight of the United States armed forces backing him, and that was gone now. It was a feeling of safety and security he had taken for granted and now cause for concern to have lost it.

"Don't be offended now, Charlie, but before we go anywhere, you are walking through the x-ray scanners which identify Krys agents. I hope you understand."

"Has every one of our Regiment been through them?"

Taylor nodded.

"Then I should not like to be the odd man out."

Fifteen minutes later they stood before Dupont and several other EA representatives. Taylor wondered if anyone else ever got such dangerous and specialist missions. The wars had been fought on many fronts and by many millions of people, but all he saw is what was before his own eyes.

"Today is the day we have our opportunity to end this war," stated Dupont. "Not through weight of arms, not through a wonder weapon, or by casualties inflicted and lost, but by knowledge. This war was not started by humans, and yet we fight one another all the same."

He looked around to all standing before him, as they nodded in agreement and hoped that such a plan could work.

"The meet shall take place in Basel at 1500 hours. Colonel Taylor, you are to act as representative of the EA, and as such will intend no violence while under the banner of peace, unless violence is conducted against you."

"And should we expect it?"

"I hope not, Colonel. We have to pray common sense still prevails among our former comrades-in-arms, but I would not rule out the possibility of an attempt against you. With your name and reputation, you are an invaluable representative for us, but also a key target for our enemy."

"So I'm being used as bait?"

"No, Colonel. I am placing you in danger, as I believe your name and reputation may be enough to sway officers who may otherwise not be swayed."

More ways of saying I'm getting fucked both ways, he thought. Taylor didn't like any of what he was hearing.

"You can't honestly believe this can work?" he asked dubiously.

"I do," snapped Dupont. "It is what we have been working for long and hard week after week so that we can save lives, thousands, maybe even millions. If the Krys are setting us upon one another, it is only in order divide and conquer, and we cannot let that happen. Or do you not consider your life worth risking for the potential of saving millions?"

It was hard for Taylor to argue with that. He just wished it were someone else's neck on the line for once.

"You will take a single copter and six personnel, including yourself and a pilot to Basel, where you shall be met by an equivalent contingent sent by General Schulz. He assures me that he is sending one of his most trusted officers and guarantees your safety, providing you abide by the ceasefire that has been negotiated. You may take weapons, but be very careful about how you present yourselves. You may not fire or be seen to attempt to use your weapons, unless you are absolutely certain that your lives are in danger. I recommend you take only the coolest of minds on this one."

"Sounds like the perfect trap to capture the Colonel to me," said Jones. "Which would be a major blow to your cause and a huge victory for the UEN."

"I am aware of that problem, Captain."

"Aware of that problem?" asked Parker. "You could be sending us to our deaths, and that's all you have to say?"

"Yes, Sergeant, and I do not know why you are even present here when you lack seniority and have little to add."

"Enough!" Taylor interrupted.

Dupont was surprised he spoke out but knew they all

needed to cool off.

"Sergeant Parker is a vital asset in the Regiment, but that does not excuse her tone," he said, glaring at her. She was silenced but not at all happy.

"I send troops out every day and with a good chance they'll die," said Dupont. "I don't like it, but that's my job. In this instance, I'm risking six to save God knows how many. Good odds and a calculated risk worth taking, wouldn't you say?"

She couldn't argue with that, but emotion was getting the better of her. For she would have any others risked in the mission besides Taylor.

"I have to wonder why we can't do this remotely?"

"I wish we could, Colonel, but I do not want any chance of the information discussed to be intercepted by third parties, and there is no way to be sure of security. Additionally, you will travel with and deliver genetic material which is proof of the Krys agents."

"Genetic material?"

"Armand's head. It has everything they need to know, and we get to retain a live specimen."

"That abomination should be put down," Jones snapped.

"I can understand your feelings on the matter, Captain, but the survival of that clone is essential, the only living proof of Krys clone technology."

"On that note, I have to bring it up, but how do we

know they cannot clone any of us?"

"The official word from Rossi is we just don't know. However, Captain Jones spent considerable time as a prisoner of the enemy involving experimentation we never fully understood. Her educated guess is that they require substantial genetic material to replicate, and, or physical access to the subject."

Another load of maybes, great, thought Taylor. He looked to Charlie as they discussed the darkest time in the Captain's life, but he seemed completely disassociated with the subject.

"Taylor, you understand what is going on here better than almost anyone. I trust in you to get the point across and reinforce it with the evidence supplied to you. I wish you every luck."

Taylor nodded in agreement and left. It was one of the shortest briefings he had ever attended, which was especially bizarre, considering the importance of the endeavour they were about to embark on. As they walked away from the brief, Taylor looked to Grey. He had become his right hand man since Jones had been gone.

"Assemble the Regiment."

"Everyone?"

"Yeah, at the drill square."

"Yes, Sir," he replied and hurried off, yelling commands through his comms channel.

Parker seemed surprise at the order and looked to

Mitch for answers.

"If whoever goes on this mission doesn't return; it is important that the Regiment goes on as we intended."

"Regiment? When did that happen?"

"It's a long story, Charlie, but don't get your hopes up. It's a title awarded only in name and to give us some independence in our operations."

"What's the current strength?"

"About two hundred, give or take considering recent casualties."

"Two hundred? Not even close to battalion strength."

"Like I said."

Corporal Herrera and Silva took a pace forward simultaneously.

"That's four."

As he said, it Acosta leapt forward enthusiastically. Taylor could see he was trying to make an impression and had jumped before he had thought, but he liked that.

"Five, good."

He looked over to the copter crews who were milling about together at the edge of the circle.

"Last one needs to be a pilot to get us there, just one. We cannot spare the number for a co-pilot. Who'll it be?"

"Well, hell," said Rains. "Only one of us is crazy enough to fly you, Colonel."

He knew Eddie would be the man for the job.

"All right, that's it. I want you all to know what we're

doing here and what's at stake. We have a chance to end this war, with proof of Krys involvement being the catalyst of it all. It could all end tomorrow. Or we six could be dead, and the war goes on anyway. Should that happen, Grey will have command of the Regiment and Sgt Parker will receive an immediate field commission as Grey's second. That will be my final orders should we fall, have you all got that?"

They grunted in approval.

"I said have you got that?"

The response that came was a mixed mess of "Aye, aye, Sir!" from the marines and "Yes, Sir!" from the British soldiers amongst them. It brought a smile to Taylor's face.

"Okay, then. We've got an hour till we depart. For those coming with me, grab your gear and be ready to move. The rest of you, you're under Captain Grey's command until I return. Fall out!"

Parker came right up to him with an amused expression.

"So all it would take for me to get a commission is your death? Seems a reasonable price," she jested.

Taylor passed off the comment; his mind was too focused on the seriousness of their situation.

"If I don't come back, you must step up and be the officer this unit needs. Inter-Allied has been a key driving force in winning the wars we have had to suffer through, and it must remain so. The World looks to us for inspiration, for courage, and for resolve. If we have none, where does that leave the World?"

"But you're not gonna die, you can't."

He took her hands.

"Yes, I can. We all can. But this Battle for Earth is about more than one man. Remember that."

"Not for me it isn't," she replied.

He put his hand to her cheek, realising she truly meant it.

"You're coming back from this because I need you."

"Then I'll make it back."

His hand slipped from her cheek, and he stepped past to join the volunteers who were awaiting him.

"All right, this is a peaceful meet...supposedly. But let's just try and remember when we've ever met an enemy and got away without a fight?"

None of them had an answer.

"I want everyone in full gear. Be sure to carry a full complement of ammunition and grenades, including flashbangs, and carry a replacement load in the copter. Eddie, there are just six of us, so you're gonna have to be geared up and ready to use a rifle at a moment's notice. Not like you haven't managed before."

"Ahh yeah, I fly, I fight, I do everything, jack-of-all-trades, you know?" he replied with a grin.

"Make sure to load up smoke charges on the copter and have the door guns fitted and ready to be used if we need them."

"You expecting us to fight a whole war by ourselves?" asked Eddie.

"If need be. The rules of this encounter are no more than six personnel and one copter. That's it. Within that framework, I want every contingency we can manage."

"What about the nose guns? I can control the fixed positions while I fly, but not the chin at the same time."

"I can do that," Jones said.

"Well, right then," replied Eddie.

"Good, now remember, no matter what happens, nobody fire anything unless fired upon. We cannot risk this going to shit," said Taylor.

"We know who we're expecting to meet?" asked Silva.

"Negative, and neither have they been told who will be sent from our side."

"So what are we expecting here, for you to lay out the truth for them and what then?"

"In theory?" asked Taylor. "I lay out the facts, hand over Armand's head for them to further investigate, and they go away and make up their own minds."

"His head?" asked Silva.

"It's a long story."

"Well, okay then."

"That's about all there is to know. Lastly, if it all goes to shit, and we become scattered, it is each man for himself. We're on the border and close to friendly units. Make your way west, and be sure you have your ID cards with you to get back over our lines."

They were all content there was nothing else to ask or say, but no one was happy about the scenario. They were fighters, not negotiators or delivery boys.

"Okay, you know what you have to do. Gear up and get ready to move."

It was five minutes to the hour when Eddie was making his final flight checks around the craft, and the others drank a last coffee before embarking. The General's personal vehicle rode into view and came to a halt beside them. Dupont leapt out with a few of his staff. One carried a square sealed medical box that they knew would be the head they were to deliver. It felt both bizarre and barbaric to be delivering a head to the enemy, but Taylor accepted it was the job they had been given.

The box was handed to him. He took it and passed it on to Acosta to carry. The Private took the box with some suspicion and held it uncomfortably. Clearly, the idea of transporting a severed head made him as uncomfortable as the rest of them.

"You've got an escort up to our frontline, Taylor. You are to run landing lights and beacons from lift off until you land in Basel at the coordinates given."

"We'll be a target for every son of a bitch out there," replied Eddie.

"Those are the instructions, and I have been promised by General Schulz himself that if you comply with those guidelines, you will not be harmed."

"Well that's just fucking great," muttered Eddie.

The General didn't pick him up on it, as he knew he was asking a lot of them all.

"Sure we shouldn't have a scientist with us?" asked Taylor. "I mean I can say everything I know, but I am no expert."

"At this stage we cannot risk any of the researchers on the project. This may be intended as a peaceful gathering, but I want everyone there to be capable of handling themselves in the event of it turning ugly. Inside the box there are data cards outlining all of our findings so far, including all interviews made with Armand before his death. Along with your testimony, it is all the proof we have to make this work."

"Well, I guess there's nothing else to say on the matter."

"Other than good luck," replied Dupont, stretching out his hand to Taylor.

Time and context had changed the General in ways Taylor could never have thought possible. Never did he believe he would have accepted his hand in friendship, but he did. Not another word was spoken as they boarded the copter, and Eddie fired up the engines. Jones climbed into the co-pilot seat ready to control the chin turret if need be, but Taylor prayed he would not. As the door shut, Jones looked around to Taylor.

"I'd have thought we would have taken the Deveron

for a mission of this nature."

They all remained silent, realising Jones had been out of the loop for so long, he hadn't heard the news.

"Deveron went down when all this sparked off."

"And Ryan?"

Taylor shook his head.

"Damn shame."

They all groaned in agreement and tried not to think about the fact they were now heading into a similar shit storm as to what had been the cause of Ryan and the Deveron meeting their end. Taylor never found out what happened to Ryan. He was hurt badly but still breathing the last he saw him at the crash site. He doubted he had made it through, but it was far from impossible.

"Listen up," said Taylor. "You heard what the General had to say. Normally, I'd say to hell with waiting for the enemy to fire first, but in this case, we must follow those orders. If there is even the remotest of chances we can pull this off, then we need every possible thing in our favour to make it work."

The all accepted, but it was going to be hard to be disciplined enough to do so. Years of fighting the Mechs had taught them to always fire first as they might not get a second chance. There was nothing more to be said now. They waited until Eddie finally broke the silence with some news.

"That's it. Our support's gone, and we're heading over

no man's land."

They expected to feel the impact of a missile or gunfire at any moment, but it never came. Five minutes later he spoke again.

"Here we go. Thirty seconds and we'll be on the ground."

Like a beached whale for anyone to pick at, thought Taylor.

They put down on the roof of the tallest building in the town as arranged, so both parties could feel safe that they were at least not being watched from the ground. Though after their recent drone attack, Taylor didn't feel safe at all.

"Eddie, you stay at the controls unless I say otherwise. Keep scanning the skies for all craft and report anything suspicious."

"Got it."

"Rest of you, with me. Act casual, but be ready for anything."

He stepped up to the door and hit the open button. The ramp slid down to the rooftop, and he could see six human soldiers awaiting them. He stepped out first with Acosta close behind and lugging the box they had come to deliver. Their welcoming party stood before a ship much like they had arrived in, and a UEN Major stood at the head of the group. Taylor didn't recognize him, but as he stepped out, he was greeted by name.

"Welcome, Colonel Taylor."

"That's not a good sign," whispered Taylor.

"How'd you know who was coming?" he shouted.

"I did not, but I of course recognise you."

Taylor could not pinpoint the accent, but it was of eastern European origin.

Bullshit! If he'd not known I was coming, he would have been a little more surprised.

"I am Major Saric and am personal attaché to General Schulz. He has informed me to listen to whatever you have to say, and collect any evidence you might have and take it to him personally."

"Would have been nice if he could have come here himself. This is a rather important issue which could affect the future of the human race."

"And yet they send you. Not a scientist, not an EA leader or representative or diplomat. They send you, Colonel, a combat officer."

"I guess they just trusted in my winning personality."

"So, down to business. Explain to me these wild rumours about aliens cloning humans and what evidence you have."

Taylor reached back, grabbed the box from Acosta, and launched it in place down before him. He kicked it so it slid three metres across the rooftop and stopped in front of the Major. He looked less than impressed with his etiquette.

"There are aliens among your ranks. They look like

humans, but they are here to fuel this and keep us fighting. There is no need to carry on fighting, for we only make Earth weaker and more prone to invasion once again!"

Saric looked suspiciously at Taylor and then down to the box. He knelt over it and twisted the locks until the seal broke. He hinged back the lid. A mist arose as the frozen contents met with the warm afternoon air. As it cleared, Saric reached in and took out the head as if not phased by the barbaric gesture.

"You have your people check into this, and you will quickly find that head belongs to something not entirely human. The Krys are fucking with us here, and we're playing right into their hands," pleaded Taylor.

"Councillor Armand, we did wonder who you suspected."

Taylor looked confused for a moment, as he tried to make sense of what Saric had said.

"You see, Colonel, we know Armand was a Krys clone. We know because he was one of us," he said as he stood up and grinned wickedly.

It was just the trap Taylor had expected and prayed would not be the case. He lifted up his comms. "Rains fire her up, now!" The turbines were whirling within two seconds, but just as Taylor turned to move something struck the roof of the copter, and the power cut out immediately.

"What the fuck!" Rains shouted. Taylor looked up to

the cockpit and could see Rains was panicking as he tried to no avail to make the system work.

Taylor looked back to Saric. Several other figures came up from the stairs behind him. His face turned to disgust on recognising the military police insignia on US Marine Corps uniforms.

"You are under arrest, Colonel Taylor!"

With that, he heard the roar of engines and two craft swooped in. Saric was reaching for his gun, and Taylor had heard enough.

"Run!" he screamed.

He got to a sprint towards the far edge of the rooftop, and the others had not hesitated to follow him. Gunshots rippled the floor at their feet, but they had reached the edge, and Rains had leapt out his copter and caught up. Taylor launched himself off the rooftop in what felt sickening; he had to trust in his equipment. He had no other choice.

As he hit the open air and dropped like a stone, his boosters started to kick in and he could see just how high they were.

"What the hell happened?"

"It was a trap, Eddie!" replied Taylor.

"Well, thanks, you just lost me another bird!"

"I'll be sure to note it in the report if we make it back!"

He knew the distance they had to descend was pushing the limits of their suits and would be all the juice they had if they did make it. He heard an engine roar overhead; a gunship was descending towards them.

"Oh, hell!"

He lifted his rifle and fired but couldn't get any accuracy with the turbulence.

"Into the building!"

"You what?" screamed Rains.

"Bank now!"

Taylor banked hard into the side of the building they had leapt from and fired a burst of shots at the reinforced glass they were heading for. It was just enough to weaken it a little as he put his arms up in front of himself for protection and hurtled through the glass, sliding ten metres into an office. There was no finesse to it, and he landed hard.

"Everyone here?" he asked.

He looked around to see only four of his comrades were in sight.

"Who's missing? Rains?"

"Yeah, I'm here."

"Silva?"

"Here."

"Acosta?"

"Here."

"Jones?"

No response came.

"Jones!" Taylor shouted again.

They heard the thunder of boots rushing towards them. He turned back to the window they had come from in the hope they could once again make a jump, even if it would mean leaving Jones behind. But as he made a step to do so, the gunship raised into view completely blocking they path.

"Whose clever idea was this, again?" Eddie asked as Silva helped him to his feet.

Taylor looked at the gunship and noticed it was in US markings. He knew he could use that to his advantage as he turned around to oppose those coming for them. Taylor didn't try and run for cover or raise his weapon when several troops burst into the room. They were all MPs with their rifles held high and screaming at the tops of their voices. It didn't intimidate Taylor or his team; they looked unbothered by their presence.

Through the middle of the MPs strode an officer. He walked with an arrogance and self-importance that made Taylor think they had met before, but then there were so many MPs like him, it was hard to tell.

"Colonel Taylor, you are under arrest for the charge of absence without leave, and insubordination, along with a series of other charges to be determined prior to your court martial. You are to lay down your weapons and come with us."

"And if I don't?"

"I have been instructed to inform you that should you

come peacefully, charges will only be made against yourself, while your collaborators will suffer only a warning. Should you not come peacefully, your entire outfit will be put to court martial, including all who remained in the United States throughout."

What a bastard!

Taylor could see the man was a Major, and he didn't like the fact he hadn't shown the courtesy of introducing himself, but he let it slide in the hope of getting through to the man inside.

He is a marine, after all.

He thought it was worth a shot to try and make the officer see sense.

"Do you know what is at stake here, Major? Do you realise what we're trying to accomplish here? We have a chance to end this war. A war that the United States will get dragged into, whether it wants to or not. You have a chance to help us end it all here."

"It's not my job to interfere with the politics of the World, Colonel, and neither is it yours. We have rules for a reason, and when you signed up to the Corps, you signed on to abide by those rules."

"Fuck sake, Major! Pull your head out of your ass and open your eyes. This is about more than your shitty little job!"

He knew as the words were coming out of his mouth they would do nothing to sway the man's mind, but he was infuriated by what he was hearing.

"You have five seconds to lay down your weapons," he replied.

"Five...four..."

"Be smart, Major. This will not end well!"

"Three...two..."

The Major was halted by the sound of an object bouncing across the floor and landing in the middle of the MPs.

"Grenade!"

Taylor went to ground as the MPs leapt for cover, but the room ignited into a blinding light, accompanied with a deafening explosion. As Taylor looked up, he could see a few of the MPs stumbling around trying to come to their senses, but smoke was flooding the scene from a second grenade. Taylor turned to see the gunship pilot didn't know what to do because he couldn't fire into both groups. Through the smoke came a few muzzle flashes as bullets riddled two of the MPs, and Jones burst out of the smoke.

He didn't stop but rushed on and past Taylor towards the gunship. Taylor watched in astonishment as Jones fearlessly leapt out of the building and launched himself at the cockpit of the ship. The pilot realised too late what was going on, and Jones hit the windshield full force. The glass half caved in, leaving Jones embedded in the nose. The pilot reached for a sidearm, but he grabbed him by his helmet and smashed his head forward onto the console three times until his face was a bloody mess. The copter began to dip and spiral out of control.

"Let's go!" Taylor ordered.

The whole group sprinted for the opening and leapt after the falling copter. They saw Jones leap from it just as it collided with the same building and burst through the glass as it erupted into flames.

They came to a smooth landing shortly after and looked up to see and tail of the gun ship still half protruding from the building.

"You're a crazy son of a bitch, you know that?" Taylor asked Jones.

"Yeah, well I can't let you have all the glory."

Taylor shook his head in disbelief. He knew the chances of that working were pretty slim, and it brought a smile to his face that they had pulled it off.

"Why don't they jump after us?" asked Herrera.

"Because they're a bunch of pussies," replied Silva.

Taylor looked around at the empty street. They had landed in a small loading bay area behind a block of buildings in the main high street of the town. They could hear the traffic running parallel with them as if nothing had happened.

"We gotta move. They'll be on our asses soon enough," said Taylor.

They rushed around a bend heading towards the road

and found a limousine, parked with a driver sitting on the bonnet and drinking a coffee. The man looked at them. He was surprised but made no attempt to move.

"You!" Taylor shouted and pointed to the man.

He seemed surprised and replied in a language Taylor didn't understand.

"We're taking your car," Taylor added, pointing his rifle at the man.

Finally, he replied in English and put his hands up as if to surrender.

"I won't stop you."

He stepped aside and out of their way.

Taylor climbed into the driver's seat, but it was a tight fit with all of his gear on.

"We're getting out of here in style," he said, putting his foot to the floor. The rear wheels spun before Silva had even pulled the back door shut.

CHAPTER FIVE

"Right!" Herrera shouted. "That way! That way!"

"Will you shut up, fucking backseat driver!"

He took the bend anyway and could see the signs for France.

"UEN forces and US MPs operating in Switzerland. If they both had permission to operate there, things really have gone to hell," said Jones.

Taylor nodded in agreement.

"Anyone know how far our lines are?" asked Silva.

"You mean you didn't check that sort of information before we left?" asked Taylor.

"I'd kinda expected to be flying out."

"Rains, what the hell happened up there?"

The pilot shrugged. "All I know is something struck the body of the copter, and two seconds later, bam, no juice. Must be some kind of power jammer."

"And if that thing had hit us in the air?"

"We'd have dropped like a stone."

Acosta's face was one of shock. The scenario terrified him.

"All right, we've got enough to worry about right now," said Taylor. "We're heading for the frontlines from the wrong way, and we aren't exactly inconspicuous."

"I know Dijon is still with us," said Herrera.

"Dijon? Taylor asked. "That's what, a hundred klicks away? Well it's a start."

Border control signs lay ahead, and Mitch could already see armed military personnel manned them.

"How come that Saric isn't on our arse yet?"

"I figure it'll take them a little while to identify this vehicle, Jones, but not too long once we go through this border."

"Any ideas how we're gonna get through?"

There was almost no traffic trying to get over the border, just a single military column stopped off and waiting to pass through in a single lane.

"There's no way they'll let us through once they see our uniforms, let alone if they recognise us," said Silva.

"Then to hell with it," replied Taylor.

He put his foot to the floor, and the limo surged forward with what was clearly a substantial engine. The heavy beast of a vehicle surged forward towards a gate between two booths. Two of the soldiers turned in surprise and started to swing their rifles off their shoulders. As they did, he heard a clunk on the roof and looked in the rear view. He saw Silva and Herrera step out through a sunroof. The guards took aim but were riddled with shots as the two of them peppered the area around them.

Soldiers all around were rushing to their vehicle to get weapons which had been stowed or laid about as they rested at the side of the road, never expecting to be shot at so far behind their lines. Dozens scurried about to try and stop them, but it was too late. The limo hit the barrier and smashed it aside as though it weighed nothing at all.

Silva turned and fired a burst from where they had passed at two soldiers taking aim and ducked back inside the car.

"Wohoo!" he yelled.

He was like a kid at Christmas.

"Top ten things to do in life, run a border!" he shouted and kept laughing.

He stopped when he saw a column of armoured vehicles ahead; Mechs marched beside them. The sign they passed said they were on the road to Mulhouse.

"Mulhouse? Where the fuck is that?"

Jones was frantically punching buttons on his Mappad, trying to make sense of where they were. They passed the rows of vehicles in the hope no one would start shooting. The dark glass of the massive car was the only protection they had from identification.

"We can't stay on this road," said Taylor. "Only a matter of time till word gets along the line. They're probably putting up road blocks, right now."

"Are we really that important to them?" asked Herrera.

"Well maybe not you, but the rest of us are," replied Jones with sarcasm.

The others began to laugh when Jones shouted out. "Left here!"

Taylor pulled the wheel hard, and the back end of the stretched wheelbase slid around and smashed into a lamppost on the corner of the bend they wanted to take. The post was smashed down into the building beside it, but it had at least stopped the slide.

"Nice driving!" yelled Silva.

Taylor planted his foot once more, knowing they must be drawing attention.

"Where are we heading?"

"This is the road west to Belfort. That column we just saw must be heading for Nancy and all the fighting that's going on up there."

"You sure did your homework since you came back."

"Knowledge is power, Mitch."

Taylor nodded in agreement.

"We gotta get out of this car. Heading in the obvious direction in such a distinctive vehicle, we're on borrowed time. This thing got auto-drive?"

"Yeah, but if we ditch this ride now, we could be

overrun on foot," added Silva.

It was a tough call. Use speed to try and outrun, or stealth to try and sneak back to their lines. Taylor was just counting the seconds away until a gunship or drone hit them, and that thought alone was enough to make him want to ditch the car.

They were in a suburb now and could tell they were heading for a scenic route west. He pulled in down a narrow side road and brought them to a halt between two buildings where they would be out of sight. He got out and rested against the car. The others did the same.

"It's not possible to take the car and go on to Dijon. We can't keep it. Anyone got any great ideas on how to get us back? Preferably yesterday."

"Get me a bird and I'll take you there in no time."

"And fly over the frontlines without clearance from either side? Eddie, we'd be shot down before we came close."

They all went silent, mulling over the idea. They were so close, and yet it seemed so far from their grasp.

"Get the General on the line and get us evac'd?" asked Acosta.

"It's a nice idea, but he can't reach us here, not without a major offensive, and any transmissions we send out will be tracked immediately. No, we are on our own here."

"Then we go to ground and wait it out a while," said Jones.

They waited for him to continue.

"Think about it. They know our reputation as hard drivers. If they haven't found us in the next six hours, they'll assume we have made it out."

Taylor thought about it for a moment, and he liked the idea more and more.

"It's not a terrible idea."

"Thanks."

"Okay, get that car rolling, and we'll look for somewhere to dig in."

Jones reached in and pressed a few buttons before shutting the door. Moments later the car rolled off smoothly to carry on its route. They all watched it leave. The fifteen-metre luxurious vehicle was hard to let go of.

"That's a damn shame," said Silva.

They all groaned in agreement.

"General Dupont surely knows it's all gone wrong here. He must do something?" Acosta asked.

"How many times, Private?" asked Silva. "We are a few guys in a big war. Not only that, but this was a dangerous fucking mission to begin with. I thought that was perfectly clear. In this Regiment, when we get into shit, we get ourselves out."

Taylor carried on without another word to a street corner on a small residential area. It had only just occurred to him they had not seen a single soul since taking the bend a few streets back. He had become so accustomed to seeing abandoned towns and cities during the last war it meant little to him.

"Area must have been evacuated when the UEN crossed the border," said Jones.

They carried on down the street that felt like the kind of place you could be ambushed at any moment. A block further down the road, and Silva finally broke the silence.

"What are we looking for?"

As he said it, Taylor stopped and pointed. It was a small local bar.

"If we're gonna be playing the waiting game, we might as well do it in comfort."

"Oh, hell yeah," said Silva.

Taylor went first and opened the door. It was still stocked and tables set up as if they were waiting to open that day. Silva caught sight of a huge leather sofa and rushed over to sprawl out over it.

"Oh, man, this is the life."

Herrera went for the fridges behind the counter. He placed his hand on the door gave out a long sigh.

"No shit, they're still on and ice cold!"

He opened the door and found it lined with bottled beer, but he turned and looked to Taylor for permission to take one. Taylor nodded in approval.

"One each and that's it."

"Yes!" he replied, taking out the bottles and throwing them across the room to everyone.

It was a bizarre situation, none of them would deny, but they at least tried to make the most of it. Mitch took a seat at the back wall and put his rifle down on the table. Jones took a seat opposite him.

"How long do you want to stay here? Move out at sundown?"

Taylor looked at his watch, noting it was only a few hours away.

"How badly do you think they want us?"

"The UEN? There must be plenty among them who wouldn't want to come after us, either through some sense of respect or fear."

"You think we command that kind of presence?"

"Wouldn't you?"

Taylor had to agree, but he gotten so tired of such fame and notoriety during peacetime that he'd tried to forget.

"It's not like the last war. You haven't got some ugly alien bastard leader trying to take your head off for some insult to his family or some such. But the MPs, that's another story. They'll chase you to the end of the Earth to drag you home in chains."

"The fact they have been given authority to operate here is my greatest concern. The United States could turn the tide in this war, and the UEN is clearly doing everything they can to create strong bonds there."

"What's the plan, Colonel?" asked Herrera.

Taylor didn't know for sure himself. He was trying to

piece it all together in his head when his mind went back to the rooftop. Escape had been at the forefront of his thoughts for the last hour. Only now was he thinking of the purpose for being there in the first place.

"We can't stop this war," he muttered.

It was a grim realisation, and they were all starting to feel it. From the first shot in the war to that afternoon, Taylor had firmly believed they could bring a ceasefire and unite humanity under one banner once again, but it was not to be.

"What does that mean, Sir?" asked Acosta.

"That we're grinding ourselves down for the Krys to swoop in and take this planet for good. All the fighting we have done will have been for nothing. It's hopeless."

Jones kicked him under the table. "It's never hopeless. You of all people should know that as you've proven it enough times," he said. "So humanity is divided, so we fight each other, we always have. But let's not forget how hard we hit those alien bastards. They may weaken us, but they're already devastated themselves."

"But we have no idea what further resources they have."

"And they have no idea what human resolve is, and if they'd been strong enough to take this planet, they would have already, don't you think?"

Taylor was starting agree.

"They think this world is the paradise their race has been searching for thousands of years. If they could, they'd be here right now."

Taylor looked around and could see the dire faces of those sitting around the bar. Gone was the enthusiasm for the cold drinks they were still holding. It was replaced by a grim tone that made them all feel helpless. He knew he had to snap out of it before it destroyed the unit.

"Private," he said to Acosta.

"Yes, Sir."

"Why did you join the Corps?"

He hesitated for a moment; he had expected an order and not a question.

"Sir...I...I..."

"No pressure, just your gut feelings."

The others all turned their attention to the Private and were genuinely interested to hear his answer. Taylor was pleased he had successfully moved on from the dire situation of the World and for them to forget it for a moment.

"I lived my whole life in a town of just a couple of hundred people, Sir. Never went more than I guess about fifty klicks from my home. Then one day a Sergeant came through town with a few veterans and told me what the Marine Corps could offer me."

"And you believed him?" laughed Silva.

"The Corps has been good to me. Seen things I ain't ever expected to see ever, some bad, some good, but all new."

"You're a simple son of a bitch," said Silva.

The others laughed.

"You regret any of it?" asked Jones.

"How could I? When I missed the last war, I thought I'd missed out on the biggest thing ever happened in this world. Thought if I signed up, then maybe I might be around and not miss whatever happened next."

It was an interesting perspective and got Taylor thinking.

"Not a bad explanation," he admitted.

"Sir, and you, if you don't mind me asking. Why did you sign up?" asked Acosta.

He had to think about it for a moment.

"I honestly can't remember anymore. I can't recall ever wanting to do anything else."

"Maybe we were just born for the Corps?"

Taylor smiled. "Sounds like you should get that on a shirt, Private."

"I think I might when we get home, Sir. Think I could make some money selling 'em?"

Taylor liked the fact he knew they would be getting home; he didn't just hope for it. He wasn't sure if that was due to youthful hopefulness or confidence, but it didn't matter. Taylor was feeling better about things already. While he had his comrades at his side, they had a chance at accomplishing anything.

"We're in the middle of a war, and yet nobody knows where we are...in the wind," Jones mused.

Taylor looked around the little bar that appeared to be a long running family business. Pictures of several generations adorned the walls. He'd got comfortable now and had no desire to move. It had been a long day with an early start.

"We'll stay here the night."

"Is that wise?"

"Charlie, I figure whoever is after us will expect us to move by night. Their troops will have limited movement once the sun is down, and that'll mean we really stand out. In the day, we just look like everyone else, pretty much."

"Apart from that," Jones said, pointing to the stars and stripes patch on Taylor's arm.

He'd worn it for so many years he had forgotten it was even there. He reached around and pulled it from his sleeve and looked at the faded colours. He'd never been without it on his uniform, and it was a strange feeling he didn't appreciate. The others looked shocked, watching him stare at the patch until finally he looked up at them.

"Same for the rest of you. Get your colours off."

They reluctantly did so.

"You know without these on we could be considered spies rather than soldiers?" asked Silva.

"I think that's the least of our problems right now, don't you think?"

Taylor slipped the flag patch into a pocket out of sight and tried to act as if it didn't bother him. It occurred to him that he wasn't even acting in the service of the United States anymore, but that wasn't enough to make him take it off.

"You really think we can pass ourselves off as UEN troops?"

"Why not, Charlie? There's God knows how many nationalities involved in this."

"And if we're called up on it, who are we supposed to be?" asked Silva.

"I dunno, say you're Dutch or something. I always hear how much they sound like us when they speak English."

"Maybe to a dullard," replied Jones.

"Maybe we'll get lucky."

Taylor got up and strolled over to Silva, slumping down in one of the sofas beside him. He dared not take his armour off should they be discovered, but it was still comfortable enough he could sleep there.

"So we really staying put?" asked Silva.

Taylor nodded and began to doze off.

"Rotate watches with two on," he muttered, but he couldn't keep his eyes open any longer and was out for count.

"Sure it's a good idea staying here?" Herrera asked Silva.

"None of the options we have got are ideal, but one thing's for sure, we couldn't continue on in the state we are in. We hit things fresh tomorrow, and we'll get out of here."

"But we failed here, didn't we? Even if we do get out, it was all for nothing," said Herrera.

"The Colonel took a fair gamble which had to be taken. There are no certainties in war."

The Corporal turned to Jones who was still slowly enjoying his solitary beer and making it last.

"What do you think, Captain?"

"Jones suddenly looked up at him. His mind had been elsewhere."

"Think of what?"

"This war, how we weren't able to stop it."

"I think it's bad news, but there is absolutely no benefit in crying over what we cannot change."

"I don't believe that," said Herrera. "I've never seen the Colonel meet a challenge he couldn't overcome."

"That's a lot of faith to be putting in one man. More of a burden than I'd want to shoulder."

"But he always comes through for us, and so do you."

Jones didn't know what to say.

"And this is why the UEN wants the Colonel out of this war so badly. He's a massive boon for whoever has him. He inspires men and women to victories they never dreamed of accomplishing," said Silva.

Rains laughed. "Oh, come on, he's not a god. How about all the times I've saved your asses?"

"Agreed, we've all done a lot of good," said Silva. "But it is Taylor who's kept us together. He is an asset the

Regiment cannot afford to lose, that the EA cannot afford to lose, and that we cannot afford to lose. The United States already has, and look how hard it's trying to get him back, and they ain't even in this war."

"Yet," stated Jones, "there's only so long anyone can stay out of this."

"You really think they'll come in on it?" asked Herrera.

"Definitely, once they know which way the wind is blowing."

"You're not suggested they'd just pick the winning side?"

Rains laughed again. "Oh, come on, man."

Jones nodded in agreement as well.

"Then I guess we just gotta give the right impression," said Herrera.

The UEN has used Mechs in their armies, and that's the first point in our favour. Another few decisions like that, and the work is done for us."

"And what then, we just blow the shit out of each other till one side is still standing?" asked Acosta.

"That's about the sum of it," replied Jones. "And then that Erdogan, or whatever his name is, will come at the survivors with all he's got. That's what I would do."

Six hours later Taylor awoke to an eerily quiet room. He got up to look at his watch and was amazed to see he'd been out for so long. It was dark outside, but the streetlights were still on. He looked over to the door to see

Rains sat on guard and alert. Acosta was across the room, his rifle laying across his legs as he sat on a tabletop.

Mitch got up, and despite his body feeling stiff, he felt fresh and good. He stepped over to Rains, pulled up a chair, and sat opposite him.

"You let me sleep a long time."

"You needed it."

"I'm sorry I got you into this again. Seems half the time you get involved with us anymore, you end up with a rifle in hand."

"Was getting pretty attached to that bird too. Called her Agathe."

Taylor laughed. "Agathe? Not exactly smooth."

"Hey, named her after a lovely French girl I met a few weeks back."

Taylor held up his hands. "I take it back, and I hope that Agathe lasts a little better."

"So if we get back to our lines..."

"When, not if," Taylor interrupted.

"All right, when. What will you do then?"

"Go back to the frontline I guess. Wherever we're ordered to go."

"It'll be a waste."

Taylor waited for him to elaborate.

"Inter-Allied is something special. You can achieve things no other unit could hope to. You should be saved for more important tasks."

"What, like Special Forces, what do you think we are?"

"Look at what you have achieved. Just stop and look back at all the things you have done in the last what, six years. You are no ordinary marine, and this is no ordinary unit. Inter-Allied is something special. It always was."

"Well, thanks, but you better include yourself in that. You are one of us now, 'cos you sure ain't French Air Force."

"Hell, no!"

The night passed without incident and at 0600 hours in the early morning, as things were just beginning to warm up, Jones stepped out of the front door to take in the fresh morning air. Taylor moved to join him.

"So what now?"

"We need to blend in. Head back north to the main road, disguise ourselves among the troops there, and make our way to the frontline."

"Risky business."

Taylor nodded in agreement. Now he was recovered, and able to reflect on the day before, his mind wandered to the scene when Jones had saved them and taken out the gunship.

"Yesterday, when you saved our asses," stated Taylor.

"What of it?"

"Well, a few things. One, it was batshit crazy what you did."

"Which bit?" asked Jones, seeming to pass it off as

nothing unusual.

"All of it. For one thing, you didn't hesitate to shoot those MPs. Humans who aren't even in this war, Americans."

"I didn't enjoy it, if that's what you're asking."

"No, no. That's not what I meant."

Taylor went silent, trying to find a way not to offend his friend, but Jones continued on for him anyway.

"Those MPs stood in the way of your freedom, our freedom. We gave everything for this world to remain free, what are two lives to add to the toll?"

"Well I agree...in principle. I was just surprised to see you take them down like that, without concern or anything."

"I had concern, but for us. We cannot stop to care or consider the dangers to those who oppose us and put our lives in danger. Those days are long gone. They ended the first day the Krys set foot on Earth. It's a harsher world now than it has been in hundreds of years. I tried to pretend it wasn't and turned my back on it all. But it is a fighter's world. Those who fight to survive and win have a chance, and those who do not, don't."

Taylor agreed but was surprised to hear the grim analysis of their world from Jones. For a man who had been so compassionate over the years, he now seemed to be utterly black and white.

"You know whether it was right or wrong, there'll be a price to pay for it one day?"

"Maybe, if we ever make it through any of this. Let's worry about winning this war before we worry about a few red caps getting hurt. We bled enough in these wars. About time they had a few licks themselves."

Taylor smiled. He had hated the MPs his entire life, and it always amused him to hear someone else ripping into them.

"And how about that gunship?" asked Taylor. "That was hard-core."

"I learnt it from you."

Taylor thought back and remembered doing something similar, but in space."

"All right, I'll give you that one."

Taylor looked back into the bar. They were all ready and waiting.

"Let's do this."

They headed on down the abandoned streets as if they were taking a walk in the park. Anything else would be suspicious so far back from the frontline. Finally, they came across the lamppost that had been demolished by the limo. It was the marker point for them reaching the main road. Up ahead they could see a line of trucks passing by.

"I don't like this," said Silva.

But they carried on walking as if there were no danger at all. As they stepped out to cross the road, a six-wheeled armoured vehicle rolled to a halt beside them. They froze.

Oh shit, Taylor thought.

To their surprise the driver's hatch opened, and the driver appeared before them and beckoned for them to jump on. He was shouting something Taylor didn't understand, though it sounded like German to him. Taylor couldn't believe their luck and knew they had to clamber on or risk appearing suspicious.

No soldier ever turns down a ride.

The six of them climbed aboard, and a moment later the vehicle had rejoined the convoy.

"Well what do you know? A free ride," said Silva with a smile.

Taylor was glad they were on top and didn't have to communicate with the crew, but he couldn't help but feel exposed. They were on full view to all they passed. They were on the road for close to an hour when the convoy came to a slow grind. Jones tapped Taylor's shoulder and subtly pointed to where they were heading. Mitch turned to see a line of US MPs up ahead and checking the occupants of each vehicle.

"Ah, fuck," he whispered.

"No way we'll make it past them. They know what we look like," said Silva.

Taylor looked around for possible options, but they were few. He gestured for them all to come in closer to hear what he had to say.

"We can't make it through there. We're gonna have to make a break for it. We can't be far away now. When I say, we jump and head west. As far as the troops here are concerned, we're the MPs' problem until we start shooting, so nobody fires unless you absolutely have to."

It felt like a last desperate attempt to get free, as criminals always do from the police when under pursuit, and so rarely successful.

"Once we hit the ground, you run. All of you," ordered Taylor. "You run and run until you get across the border, and if we don't meet again, it was an honour."

Taylor looked back to the MPs. Two of them were already taking an interest in the group. He knew they were on borrowed time.

"Good luck to you all," he whispered. "Now!"

He jumped from the stopped vehicle and hit the ground running. He glanced quickly to one side. He could see the MPs frantically trying to get their rifles in hand, but the six of them were already down a side street before they could open fire. He looked around to see the group was still together and following him. They took a bend and kept up a sprint, despite none of them knowing how far they were from friendly lines.

"I feel like a kid again, running from the cops!"

"Yeah, but cops don't shoot kids. These ones surely shoot marines!" yelled Taylor.

It was motivation to keep up the pace, but as they took a bend up ahead, they saw they had run themselves into a dead end with a brick industrial building that stood twenty metres high. It had been a heavy goods vehicle access road that overtime had been blocked for whatever reason.

Taylor looked down at the display on his suit. His boosters had almost no power left at all. He ran and jumped, hoping for the best, but he barely got five metres off the ground before smashing into the wall and landing hard on the concrete below.

He was quickly back on his feet and looking for anyway out, but there was none. The others all looked to him for options, but there was only one left to them.

"Take up positions and prepare to fire!"

They went thirty metres back the way they'd come to the nearest cover of a few walls and large industrial trash cans.

"So this is what it has come to?" asked Jones. "Backed into a corner by MPs. How lame."

"We aren't finished yet. Do not fire unless fired upon!"

The MPs took the bend up ahead and came into full view, but Taylor and his comrades did not fire. Their opponents quickly found any cover they could until the alleyway went silent. It became a standoff.

"This is Major Martin. You are under arrest! You are ordered to lay down your weapons immediately!"

They recognised the voice. It was the same officer who had tried arresting them the day before, and Taylor knew he would not be very forgiving after the punishment Jones had dealt out.

"You have five seconds to lay down your weapons and come peacefully!"

"You know this guy is really getting boring," said Silva.

"It's only a few cops playing soldiers. We can take 'em," said Rains.

Just as he said it, they watched in horror as a Mech strode into view beside the MPs. It was followed by a dozen more.

"Oh, shit," said Eddie.

"They must really want you out of the picture," said Jones.

The Mechs lined up in the open ready to fire.

"This is your final warning!" screamed Martin. "Lay down your arms and no harm will come to you!"

Nobody said a word.

"You have five seconds! Five...four...three..."

Taylor prayed for a miracle, but it seemed pointless, considering he'd never believed in a god to begin with.

"Two...one! Fire!"

The Mechs and MPs fired simultaneously, peppering the entire area. Taylor put his rifle around the corner of one of the huge trashcans and fired a burst. Two of the shots hit a Mech, and it tumbled down dead. He tried to fire again, but his rifle was hit and wouldn't fire. He ducked fully back into cover and pulled the rifle up close. Two shots had hit the barrel and front receiver, rendering it useless. He threw it aside and drew his pistol.

A scream rang out. He turned to see gunshots penetrate a hole in the wall and hit Rains. A few were absorbed by his armour, but one passed through his upper arm and another the side of his neck. He dropped down to the floor, trying to cup his wounds. Before anyone could do anything, a grenade flew overhead and landed between Herrera and Acosta. They turned to move out the way, but the blast still caught them. Acosta was hurled against a wall and knocked unconscious while Herrera took shrapnel to the legs and hit the ground face first.

All seemed lost, and not to the alien invaders or even their agents, but to a bunch of MPs with their Mech dogs. But then an engine roared overhead. It brought the firing to a stop. Everyone looked up to see a transport close to the size of the Deveron swoop in overhead and cast a shadow over them all. A US flag adorned the hull, and Taylor shook his head. He knew it was the end.

Several doors opened either side of the ship and troops jumped out. A few dozen landed on the rooftops either side of the alley, and twenty dropped in to where they had come to the dead end. They were indeed US troops and fully equipped in Reitech equipment.

Taylor, Jones, and Silva had their weapons trained on them but had made no attempt to fire. The troops didn't take cover or even kneel; they knew as much as Taylor did that it was over. An officer strode forward from the middle of the group without even a weapon raised. He wore Army Ranger insignia, as did all who had arrived with him, and bore the rank of Captain. He stopped ten paces from Taylor and looked down at the wounded before turning back to his troops.

"Medics!"

Taylor lowered his weapon, nodding to the others to do the same.

Medics rushed forward to help the wounded, and Major Martin came striding past the cover from the other direction.

"Thank you, Captain. We'll take it from here!"

The Captain looked up at the MP Major with a disgusted look on his face.

"You keep your filthy hands to yourself, Major!" he boomed.

Martin was stopped in his tracks and utterly shocked by the condemnation.

"Captain, need I remind you I have direct orders to detain these men and bring them back to the United States for trial?"

The Captain spat in front of the Major and replied, "Pack up and piss off."

Taylor didn't recognise the Ranger officer, but he liked him already.

"You are way out of line, Captain. Hand over the Colonel and his men and back down, or you will be placed on a charge!"

The Captain ignored him and raised his comms link and simply said, "Prepare to fire."

The Rangers at his back and along the rooftops trained their weapons on the MPs and Mechs. Martin's face turned to stone.

"You've done enough damage here. Walk away or never walk again."

Taylor could see the fear in the Major's eyes. He wasn't a fighting man and never would be. He was a bully who just got put in his place.

"You're in big trouble, Captain. More trouble than you can ever imagine."

With that the Major turned and left, and the Ranger officer knelt down and offered his hand to Taylor. Mitch couldn't believe their luck. He took his hand and was hauled to his feet.

"How did you do it? Who gave you the order to come to our aid?" asked Taylor.

"I did," stated the Captain. "If a soldier cannot come to the aid of Colonel Taylor and the Inter-Allied, then who will he help? There's a war to be fought. You know it. I know it. Every man and woman here came of their own accord and has pledged to defend this planet against all enemies, both foreign and domestic. I am Captain King, 2nd Ranger Battalion, and I am at your service."

CHAPTER SIX

Taylor was watching the world go by from the window of an aircraft once again as they made their way across France. He looked over to the seat opposite him that was occupied by King.

"You know, Captain, I prayed for a miracle down there. I prayed for a miracle, and I got the Rangers."

King laughed. "We've been called many things but never that."

"You know we went to that meet in Basel in good faith to try and bring an end to all this madness, and if anything, just made it worse."

"Was it worth trying?"

"Yes, of course, anything was worth risking for the chance of success."

"Then you made the right decision."

"You know we aren't fighting for the US here? We

pledged our service to the EA because they were willing to fight the battle which needed to be fought."

"Yeah, I get that."

Taylor pulled out his flag patch and stuck it back on his sleeve.

"But that doesn't change the fact we will always be Americans. And we fight for America, even when she doesn't know there's a fight needing to be fought."

"We're with you, Colonel, every step of the way. We didn't come out here to save your ass. We came to join you."

"And you know the shit that puts you in?"

He nodded.

"Well, you have my eternal gratitude."

He breathed out a sigh of relief before continuing. "What's it like back home with respect to feelings about this war?"

"Some want in, some never want to hear the word 'war' uttered again in their lifetimes. Some people are just blind to the facts before them."

"We need America in this fight. We need Americans in this fight. If you were willing to join of your own accord, would others?"

"If you were to step up and ask them, I think so."

"Then that is what we must do."

"How?" Silva asked.

"Where there's a will, there's a way."

He looked over to King and thought for a moment before making him an offer.

"What is your strength?" Taylor asked him.

"One hundred and twenty six," he replied confidently.

"If you fight beside us, you fight as one of us, and not as a member of the United States armed forces. The Inter-Allied Regiment is a mix of all sorts, the best kind of mongrel there ever was. If you would accept it, I would be honoured to have you and your Rangers form a Company in the Regiment, with you at the head."

Taylor offered out his hand as a gesture of good will to seal the deal, and King took it with a huge smile on his face.

"I can't think of an officer I'd rather serve under, even if he is a marine."

"Then it's done. Welcome to the Regiment. You can formally announce it when we land."

"Screw that," he replied.

He lifted up his comms to the entire Ranger unit. "Listen up! We just joined Taylor's Inter-Allied. Welcome to the Regiment, boys!"

A cheer rang out through the ship that was followed by a hive of conversation as they excitedly discussed their new role. Five minutes later they were coming into land at Meaux, and Taylor could not feel more relieved as they touched down. The mission had been a failure and far more arduous than expected, but Taylor could not help but feel triumphant returning safely with all he had taken out and now with a veteran Ranger Company at his command.

He was the first out of the ship down the ramp towards General Dupont who was awaiting him.

"Mission was a complete failure," he stated before he'd even reached the General. He wasn't at all surprised.

"I know, but you did your best, Colonel, I know that. Right now, I have your General White on hold. He says the US President wants to talk to you, Colonel, and I cannot state how important it is you try and get the US on board. Do whatever you have to, but get the US on side. Follow me."

Taylor's relief and excitement for having got back, and with the Rangers in tow, was completely dissipated as he was led inside an office.

"I am no negotiator."

"You're our best hope here, Colonel. And what is it you always say, adapt and overcome?"

"Improvise and overcome."

"That's it, then you know what to do."

"Gee thanks," he replied as the screen flicked on in front of him. It was General White, just as he had been told. Taylor did not greet him and just waited for the shit storm that was coming, but he was surprised to see White's tone was nothing as he expected.

"Colonel Taylor, glad to see you are alive and well."

You changed tactics on me, you son of a bitch.

"No thanks to the dogs you sent after us," he replied venomously.

"Yes, I must apologise for Major Martin. He has a heavy handed approach, but he gets the job done."

"Not this time, he didn't," Taylor snapped.

"Quite, and I do apologise for that. Martin was not given permission to use force."

"Not use force? He had Mechs blowing the shit out of us."

"Yes, and Major Martin will pay a heavy toll for his sins, just as we all must."

Great, here he goes again.

Taylor was expecting another lecture, followed by a plea for him to return to the States, but it did not come.

"Colonel, let me get to the point."

"Please do..."

"President Robinson has personally requested to talk to you. Will you receive him?"

"Yeah, go on," replied Taylor with no enthusiasm at all.

He was transferred to a secretary. "Please hold for the President."

"So much for waiting to talk with me," muttered Taylor.

The President suddenly appeared before him, and he had no idea if he'd heard his last comment or not.

"Mr President," he said.

Robinson was young for a US President and in good shape. He was clearly at least part South American descent and was slick in his appearance, but it didn't impress Taylor.

We need a fighter in office, not a suit.

"Colonel Taylor, may I just say it is an honour to finally speak to you, and may I extend the nation's gratitude for all you have done for this great nation."

Great, a kiss ass as well. This isn't gonna end well.

"Thank you, Sir," he replied, trying to remain calm.

"Colonel Taylor. You have done more for your country than can ever be asked of a man. However, I must now ask that you return home. You will not be charged. You will not face a court martial. I shall see to that. You are stepping on a lot of toes, Colonel, and straining many diplomatic relations which have taken many years and much work to set up."

"I'm sorry I am making diplomatic relations tough in order to keep the World safe," he replied sarcastically.

The President brushed his comment aside and continued.

"Do you not think this country has suffered enough in recent years? Do you not think we deserve peace?"

"Peace? I am fighting because we do deserve peace, and it must be fought for just as the founding fathers of our nation knew it."

"This is not the way, Colonel. If you..."

Taylor reached for the transmission button and cut him off. The door beside him burst open, and Dupont flew through it.

"You just hung up on your President!"

"He is no President of mine," snarled Taylor. "When a man with the balls for the job takes over, I'll talk again."

"What have you done?"

"Didn't you hear it? That asshole can't be talked into war. He's just doing everything he can to get me back there. Is that what you would have? Would you have me sent home where I would almost certainly be stripped of my rank and imprisoned?"

Dupont shook his head.

"No, I would not wish it, and you know I would take back all that I ever did to you if I could."

"This isn't about us, General. You stand beside me, and for that you are my friend."

It brought a surprised and puzzled expression to Dupont's face.

"So what now?" asked Taylor.

"I know the mission failed, but I need to know why. We need to understand this war. I need you debriefed immediately before you take your leave."

Taylor sighed. It was going to be a long day. When he finally stepped out into the open air once again, he found the sun was almost down. He felt utterly exhausted having sat for so many hours outlining all he had seen and experienced to Dupont and other EA officers. He turned and was pleasantly surprised to find Parker sitting on a wall waiting for him. Her head was down in her hands, and she looked utterly bored.

"Evening," he said softly.

Her head shot up at the sound of his voice, and she rushed into his arms.

"You know, back home they frown on this kind of behaviour, Sergeant," he said with a straight face.

"Well, we set the rules now."

It wasn't far from the truth, but he also recognised it was a potentially dangerous position to be in.

"So, did you convince the UEN to halt the war?" she asked.

Taylor sniggered. "No, it was a complete cluster fuck."

"I figured as much."

"Your vote of confidence is overwhelming."

"So what's next?"

"No idea. Just wait on new orders, I guess."

"There's no way we can end this war with the info we now have?"

He shook his head.

"With Krys agents having infiltrated the UEN at every level, there is no chance."

"And they only infiltrated the UEN, what about our side?"

He shook his head. It didn't bare thinking about, but the clone of Jones was a nasty shock and reminder of what they could be facing.

* * *

Taylor awoke and shot up as a brainwave had struck him during the night. Eli groaned beside him and was clearly not impressed with having been awoken so abruptly, but he was too single-mindedly focused to notice or care. He jumped out of bed and pulled on his clothes while she still grumbled.

"Come on back to bed. We don't have to be up for hours."

"No, the war won't wait for us," he replied.

"What?" she muttered as she turned over and went back to sleep.

He looked at his watch. It was almost 0900 hours, and they had slept way past what a marine should.

"Goddamn it."

He rushed to the door, stopping as he remembered the last time he went out without a weapon and quickly rushed back, grabbed his sidearm, and strapped it about his waist.

"Got it, I got it you son of a bitch," he muttered to himself as he strode for Dupont's office that was located in the bastion they called a research facility. As he approached, he noticed it was named only 13E.

A subtle name to conceal a mammoth structure, he thought.

He rushed into Dupont's office and found him meeting with two Generals from other EA nations.

"I need to put out a broadcast," he demanded.

Dupont stood up, shocked by his abrupt entrance.

"You will have to excuse Colonel Taylor. Combat fatigue has made him forget his manners," he said; the other two laughed.

"If the UEN won't listen to the evidence we put before them, and the US President won't see sense, let me broadcast it to the World. People trust me. God knows why, but they do. Let me take the evidence we have to every news agency in every country which still remains neutral, and let the people decide for themselves."

Dupont sat back down silently and mulled over the idea. One of the other Generals finally answered.

"Why not? It could work."

He spoke in a strong Spanish accent. Dupont shook his head and replied.

"It's a dangerous proposition. We are looking for allies, and such a thing could turn people against their governments who would blame us for inciting any trouble which ensues."

"And?" asked Taylor. "Are we not past the point of politics and simply trying to win by any means?"

"There are always politics, Colonel. Believe me, I wish there weren't. Many times have I wished I could be in your shoes and not have to play the politics game."

"Let me do it. Not with any support, given or intended by you or any member state of the EA. Let me do it as a United States Marine, as a free man. If we can get this evidence out to the people of this world who are beyond the control and indoctrination of Krys agents, we could completely turn this around."

"And if it doesn't? What if it backfires and it sounds like crazy talk? No matter how true the evidence we have, it sounds crazy."

"I can't change the truth. I can only tell it like it is."

Dupont thought about it for a moment and looked at the other two. They both nodded in approval.

"Then do it, and let us pray the audience are as passionate and trusting as you believe."

"Thank you, this is gonna work. It's gonna work like you could never believe."

"It's hardly the way to do things as far as diplomacy goes, but hell. Whatever we're doing now isn't gaining any more support. See my secretary on the way out. She will set you up with everything you need, including our press officer Captain Bernard."

Taylor was excited but also terrified that so much now depended on him. But this wasn't the pressure he was used to. He didn't have to succeed through combat, but through communication.

What the hell have I got myself into?

Half an hour later, he stood around a table with his own senior officers and the press officer as promised, but none of them yet knew his plan.

"Bernard, I am told you have plenty of contacts in the

International press?"

"Yes, Monsieur," he replied.

"Good. I need you to get me on air, live. The US is absolutely essential, so try and get a sensible hour. We've got about seven hours until the Eastern seaboard wakes up and turns on the news. When they do, I want them to see me on screen telling it to them straight."

"And what is it you will be telling them?"

"That isn't your concern, right now."

"Begging your pardon, Colonel, but if I am to negotiate this for you, the stations will want to know why. It's a big ask."

"Then tell them Colonel Taylor of the Immortals has news the World needs to hear. That should be enough."

"That's it?"

"Has to be. We need this to be last minute. If the wrong people get wind of it, they will shut us down. I need you to get us on air quickly."

"If I may make a suggestion, Colonel."

"Sure."

"Is what you are going to say controversial?"

"Yes."

"Will governments want to block it?"

"Yes."

"And will people talk about it? Will it spread from one to another?"

"Yes, I hope so."

"Then forget the mainstream media. If you want to go viral, we can post it ourselves, and the news agencies will soon pick it up before there is any chance of shutting it down."

It was a concept he had heard of, but wasn't awfully familiar with.

"Trust me, no need to live record. You put a video together, and if it's half as controversial as you think it is, the World will know about it before this day is over."

"All right, then I need a cameraman."

"What is the location?"

"The clone's cell. Behind the mirrored glass so that the camera may see him, but he cannot interfere."

"And all this is cleared by General Dupont?"

"We have free rein to do whatever the hell we want."

An hour later Taylor and Jones sat in the room as planned and ready to go. Taylor knew it wasn't being shown live, but the fact it would go out to so many so soon gave him the jitters all the same. He looked to the cameraman.

"When I say you roll, you do so until I say stop, okay?"

The man nodded in agreement.

"We're gonna put this out as is. No fancy cutting, editing, or any of that shit. This is gonna hit 'em straight."

He turned to see Jones staring at his clone. It hadn't occurred to Taylor that despite it being big news, his friend had never seen it for himself.

"Cloning? I used to read about it and thought it was fascinating. I used to joke to my mates at Sandhurst if we ever got to cloning, I would have ten of myself cloned so I'd finally have someone worth talking to."

"Wow, bet your mates really loved you."

"I think maybe the humour is lost on Americans."

"If that's what British humour is like, you can keep it."

That at least brought a smile to his face.

"If they cloned me once, how do you know they won't do it again? Maybe they already have."

"Probably. But they have played their hand and it failed. We're wise to it now."

"But how do you know I am...well me, right now?"

"I had you scanned on the way through, and I am working on getting you scanned, as well as everyone else in the Regiment every single day. God knows what possibilities there are for infiltrating us, and we cannot have it happen again."

"But do you think it's wise me staying in the unit when it is such a danger?"

"Bullshit. They could clone any one of us. I need you. The Regiment needs you. Don't tell me you're having second thoughts about fighting."

He shook his head.

"I couldn't face Coco and tell her I'd quit. I'm in this till the very end of the fighting."

"Better make that sooner rather later, okay?"

"Do my best."

"Ready when you are," said the cameraman.

Taylor knew he could have as many takes as he liked, but he didn't have the patience for a second take. He looked to Jones who looked more comfortable with the whole thing than he did.

"I'll do the talking. You're just here to look pretty."

"I always was the more handsome one."

He looked into the cell. The clone stared into their room as if he knew they were there. "Still freaks the hell out of me to see that thing that looks like your twin."

"Just say the word, and I'll end its miserable life."

"Love to, believe me. Let's do this," he turned to the cameraman. "Roll the camera."

He was given the thumbs up, and for a moment he remained silent. He looked at the floor, trying to think over how he could appeal to the World's population, and then in a moment of clarity, he just opened up and spoke his mind.

"This is Mitch Taylor, Colonel in the Inter-Allied Regiment, and hopefully still the United States Marines Corps. I currently fight for the European Alliance in a war that I know has to be fought. While some nations choose to stay out of this war, I feel it my duty to inform you, the taxpaying voting public of your respective nations, of what is truly going on here."

He looked over to Jones who seemed fairly impressed

and that spurred him on to continue.

"What you need to know is that the war currently fought in Europe is not a simple war between two Earth alliances. It is not just a human war, and I need to show you how."

He pointed for the cameraman to pan over to Jones.

"This is my good friend and fellow officer, Captain Charlie Jones. A man who has served his country and this Earth with distinction since the first invasion, and at a massive personal cost, I must add. Captain Jones, do you have any siblings?"

"No," he quickly replied.

"Let that be known. Captain Jones is an only child. Now can you please focus on the subject behind this screen with Captain Jones still in frame."

He did as requested.

"The man this side of the glass is the same Charlie Jones I have known for as long as I can remember. What you see inside that cell looks identical to Jones. It shares the same genetic make up, and is for all intents and purposes the same man. And yet, the man in that cell murdered a number of staff on this base and tried to keep a very real secret from you. The aliens we thought were beaten; they weren't beat at all. Bloodied and weakened yes, but far from beat."

He pointed for the camera to come back to him, and the cameraman quickly obliged.

"Alien agents are among us. Human clones that are almost indistinguishable from the friends, family, and neighbours we have known our entire lives. This is not a time to become suspicious of all those around you, but to stand together. The Krys, the alien invaders, will take this world again, and they are doing so under the name of the UEN. They are fighting us from within. We tried to stop this war, but that was impossible. We have just one choice left, to win it. The United States will not choose a side, nor will many others. I am here to tell you that we don't fight for a country; we are fighting for our planet. We fight for Earth and the existence of the human race. Your leaders may not see sense, but you can be the judge. We need fighters to fight for this world. Join us, before it is too late."

He looked over to Jones for approval, and he nodded in response.

"All right, that'll do."

The cameraman cut the recording and asked, "All that really true?"

Taylor nodded in response.

"Shit."

"That about sums it up."

Taylor looked back to Jones. "What d'ya think?"

"Well it was corny as hell, but the yanks will love it."

Taylor led them out of the room to where Bernard was waiting them.

"That was quick," he said in surprise.

"Easy when you know what you want to say," he replied. "As I told your man here, I don't want any fancy cuts or editing. I don't want anyone claiming the video is fake for whatever stupid reasons."

"They will anyway if it becomes popular enough."

"Well, no matter. Do your thing, whatever that is."

"Gladly."

Mitch was still dubious that anything could come of such a simple self-published video, but it required so little effort and resources, he was willing to give Bernard the benefit of the doubt.

"You've got twenty-four hours," said Taylor. "If it hasn't worked by then, we go with my plan."

Bernard was already watching the video on a screen nearby and was utterly engrossed with it. It reached the shot of the clone, and he was flabbergasted.

"I'd heard rumours about this, is it really true?"

"Unfortunately," replied Jones.

"This is going to blow peoples' minds," he stated.

Taylor nodded and left it with him.

As they strolled out of the building into the daylight once more, Jones asked, "You know you have just incited rebellion in your own country, as well as probably countless others."

"If governments can't handle the truth, on their heads, so be it."

Jones smiled. "Viva la revolution."

Hours later Taylor sat about a large maintenance bay where his unit had taken shelter from the sun, awaiting their next assignment. They all accepted that leave was a thing of the past. Most were cleaning weapons and equipment, including Taylor. His rifle was new off the shelf, since his old one required extensive repairs. He stripped the new weapon to every last component part and adjusted and reassembled it to his own configuration.

A large screen projection at one end of the hall had an Earth news channel playing; a United States endorsed and funded station that acted under the guise of neutral politics, despite few knowing its true identity. Most of the day's stories had been covering sport. It seemed bizarre while those who watched it were living in a war zone.

"I guess the US really doesn't want involvement in this war?"

"I don't think anybody wants to be involved in this war, Charlie. They just haven't realised yet that they have no choice but to be," replied Taylor.

"Colonel Taylor!" came a call.

His grip reached for his sidearm instinctively. He looked up. An officer stood before him, silhouetted against the light coming through a ceiling light. He covered his eyes from the glare and recognised Becker, the German tank commander. Taylor leapt to his feet. He could see the German flag Becker had always worn with pride was gone, replaced with a black double-headed eagle encased in a vivid yellow shield. He wasn't at all familiar with the symbol.

"What the hell are you doing here?"

"I might ask you the same question."

"No, but I mean really, why are you here? Your country is at war with France."

"No, the German government is at war with France and certain idiotic creatures with it. I still fight for Germany in the only way I can. Took me a little while to convince the EA I was genuine, but here I am."

Taylor was still looking at the symbol on Becker's sleeve, and the Captain felt he needed to explain.

"Holy Roman Empire," he stated. "It's how I can still fight as a German, without being shot for being one."

Taylor laughed. "Honestly, I'm amazed to see you are even still alive."

"Likewise."

Becker's attention suddenly turned, and his eyes looked past the Colonel to the end of the room.

"Looks like you are creating quite a stir."

Taylor looked confused. He turned to find out what the Captain meant and was met by his face projected on the massive screen.

"No way," he whispered.

"Turn it up!" Jones shouted out.

A moment later, he was listening to his own voice as

recorded earlier that day on one of the most watched news stations in the World. He couldn't believe his eyes.

"It's the Colonel!" one of the unit shouted. "Get a look at the Colonel!" another one called out. Cheering rang out and swallowed up the sound from his interview, but it was okay, he didn't need to hear it.

"What have you got yourself into, Colonel?" asked Becker.

"Long story, but in essence, we need more people like you. Volunteers to fight for what needs to be fought for."

Silva walked over to join them with a huge grin across his face. "Man, White is gonna be pissed."

"Well, I can't keep everyone happy."

Most of the Regiment was in the huge room and beginning to chant his name with excitement. He knew he had to get up and talk to them. He climbed up onto a nearby table and lifted his hands. Silence quickly followed.

"Every man and woman among you joined me in this war because you knew it was the right thing to do. Our government, our Generals, they still sit on the fence while we fight and die. Today, I am giving every American and every other nation's citizens a chance to decide for themselves!"

Becker leaned over to Jones.

"How does he do it?"

"What?"

"Survive, after pissing off so many people, and remain

so fiercely popular?"

Jones shook his head for he didn't rightly know. "It is quite amazing."

The video interview replayed again on the screen until finally it was cut short and went back to a news desk. The crowd booed but were silenced by Silva's booming voice hollering, "Quiet!"

They were all fixated on the screen now and watched as the news anchor was clearly receiving notes through a hidden earpiece before relaying them on air. The anchor was a well-dressed blonde in her late thirties and always looked one hundred percent confident in her presentation, except for this time. She looked uneasy with what she was hearing and hesitated for a moment before speaking with a slightly shaken voice.

"We have had a request from the White House for an immediate broadcast from their location...Going now live to the White House..."

The familiar White House conference room set appeared before them, but it was empty. A few moments later a man stepped up to the podium, but nobody recognised him. He was in his early thirties and Hispanic. It was clear he was prepped for the interview but was doing his best to appear confident.

"Thank you, Ladies and Gentlemen, for appearing on such short notice. I am Rodrigo Vidal, and I am advisor to the President. I am here on the President's behalf to ask for calm and consideration at this time. I am sure all of you have by now seen the broadcast put out a few hours ago by what appears to be Mitch Taylor. Let me remind you that Colonel Taylor is currently AWOL from the Marine Corps, and is acting of his own accord. We have no authentication of the videos source, nor any evidence that any material therein is accurate."

He took in a deep breath, and not one of the members of the press interrupted him as they waited with baited breath.

"The United States has seen no evidence of cloned humans or Krys involvement in the war currently being fought in Europe and its surrounding area. We have no choice but to declare this video a hoax. I repeat, the President has asked for calm consideration during this troubling time in the World. Thank you. That will be all."

Reporters jumped to get his attention, but he carried on as quickly as he could.

"Fucking asshole," said Silva. "A hoax? Get the President here, and we'll show him a fucking hoax."

"He's just towing the line. That video was never targeted at the government. It was for everyone else."

The troops were heckling the screen as it returned to the news anchor.

Becker was stunned. "You...you really just did that? That really was you who put that out there?"

Taylor nodded.

"Think it'll work?" asked Jones.

"We can only hope."

"If this evidence exists, why not get it out to the World?" asked Becker. "Why not make everyone see it to be true? Hell, even take it to the UEN. They can't understand the shit they've gotten themselves into."

"It's what we've been trying to do, and yes we tried that as well. Nearly cost us our lives. No, there is no negotiation to be had with the UEN anymore. Maybe we can get a few individuals like you to cross over, but this war will only end when we win it."

"So what now?" asked Silva.

"Wait and see. Worst case, is nothing at all."

"Colonel Taylor!" a voice boomed.

He turned to see General Dupont standing before him. *Oh, shit!*

"When did getting the evidence out to the World include open recruiting of citizens from neutral countries?"

Taylor shrugged his shoulders and stayed calm.

"You just did what none of my advisors would dare do, and what a job you did. Governments are panicking. Discussion of clones and alien involvement is spreading like wildfire. I didn't believe it ever could have worked."

"Just gotta have a little faith, Sir."

"We all knew you could fight, but who could ever have known you were capable of anything like diplomacy."

"I wouldn't call it that," he replied.

"Whatever you want to call it, you just stirred up the hornets' nest, Taylor."

"That's what I do."

Dupont walked off confidently, shaking his head in astonishment.

"When in the high hell did you get him on side?" asked Becker.

"It's a long story."

Parker appeared out of nowhere, a puzzled expression on her face.

"Never thought you had it in you," she said.

"I'm full of surprises."

CHAPTER SEVEN

Taylor awoke to a hammering on his door, causing him to leap from his bed and grab his sidearm. He rushed to the door wearing nothing but his underwear and saw Eli readying her rifle.

"Who is it?" he shouted.

"Silva!"

Taylor ripped open the door and thrust his pistol out in the face of the Sergeant Major.

"Whoa, whoa, it really is me," he complained.

Taylor looked around suspiciously outside the door before lowering his pistol.

"What is it?"

"It worked!" he said excitedly.

"What d'ya mean?"

"A Marine regiment has departed the United States to pledge allegiance to you personally, and more are sure to follow. The government hasn't been able to stop them!"

Taylor rubbed his eyes, trying to work out if he was dreaming.

"All right, give me a minute. I'll be with you shortly."

He shut the door and reached for his clothes.

"If the President wasn't pissed enough with you before, he certainly will be now," said Parker.

"So what? My job isn't to make friends and kiss ass. It's to win this war through whatever means necessary."

"Job? Are you being paid?"

He shook his head.

"Okay, it's my duty, my calling, whatever you want to call it. Hardly a time to worry about money."

"No, not when your head can get removed from your shoulders at any moment from even those close to you."

"What are you saying?"

"You need to be careful, Mitch. You may be making a lot of friends right now, but probably just as many enemies."

"Well then, you'll have to have my back, won't you?"

"Always."

He pulled on his boots and was out the door, leaving her still getting dressed.

"Way to go, Colonel!"

It was a passing soldier he'd never seen before in his life. He nodded in acknowledgement and continued on when he caught sight of a few objects in the sky. They appeared to be drones. He jumped to the nearest wall for cover and then peered around for a better look. They were drones all right, but they appeared to carry no weapons and were hovering over a drill square a hundred metres away. Out of curiosity, he made his way towards them, despite being naturally suspicious.

He took a bend and found Reiter and a few of his team standing around a pile of equipment. Acosta stood watching them. The Private noticed his arrival and beckoned for him to come forward.

"They've done it, built my idea."

Taylor looked down to see a typical Reitech rifle on a table. It appeared to be nothing out of the ordinary.

"Does it work?"

"Initial tests have been positive. We do not have any operational combat drones, so we use video surveillance models instead. The results should be near identical. Would you like to do the honours, Colonel? " Reiter answered.

"What do I do?"

"That rifle you see there is exactly as it would appear. Initially, we developed a concept weapon from the revolving launchers used in the first war, but we are well aware the carrying of additional weaponry is not ideal simply to deal with a particular target. So we redesigned the projectile so that it could be used in the current Reitech rifle. This reduces the spread of the weapon slightly, due to the calibre of the weapon, but I think you will find the results quite pleasing."

Reiter flipped open a box lying on the table. It was full of ammunition and the rounds like nothing he had seen before. The same length and diameter he was used to, but with dozens of small steel rods around the diameter of the head of the round, and initially appeared to be hollow in the centre. He pushed his finger into the hollow area, and it was actually filled with a super fine grade steel mesh.

"The metal tips disperse the round as the projectile gains velocity," said Reiter. "The mesh is exceptionally strong for its size and weight, in what can only be described as being like a spider's web. Hence the name we have been calling them, web ammunition, or web rounds if you like."

Taylor looked at the ammunition in amazement and then to Acosta.

"Your idea really did work."

"See for yourself, Colonel," he replied.

Taylor drew back the breech on the rifle and loaded a single round manually without need of a magazine. He turned and looked up at the drones that were spaced out five metres apart. He was dubious it could work, but he had faith in Reiter. He took aim and squeezed the trigger. It sounded like a half-powered round due to the low velocity. He watched in amazement as the web opened up, engulfed the first drone, and continued on to catch one behind it and then plummet to the ground.

"Well, I'll be damned."

He put the rifle down and carried on over to see the

results. The two drones were completely wrapped in the web and lifeless. One was smashed and in multiple pieces.

"So this will destroy them outright?"

"It would depend on the strength of the drone in question and the height at which it is struck. The web rounds mean the drone cannot use any stabilisation to recover itself and does land hard. With any luck, the impact will be enough to destroy the subject. The worst case is that it remains incapacitated on the ground, and therefore an easy target for you to finish off."

"It's amazing. Amazing in its simplicity."

"I can take credit for the application of the idea, but not the concept itself. That belongs to Private Acosta here, who is far smarter than it would first appear."

"We need these rounds ASAP. How quickly can you get them into production?"

"If you are happy with them as is, I can get maybe a small test batch done by tomorrow, maybe one or two hundred. Getting them into mass production may take a few weeks at least."

"Then do it. These web rounds will save a lot of lives. Make as many as you can, and get them to my Regiment immediately."

Reiter nodded in agreement and began packing away the gear to go about his work. Just as Taylor turned back to Acosta to congratulate him, his comms channel opened. Dupont was on the line.

"Colonel, report to me immediately,"

This doesn't sound good.

When Taylor got to the General's war room, he found it packed with other officers standing around a projection of Europe and all known positions of forces, both friendly and enemy.

"Colonel, your little video stunt has caused quite a stir. And while I hear rumours of whole regiments heading our way to join us, it has stirred up trouble on the frontline. Your message to the World has brought your United States ever closer to joining this war, and that has clearly led the UEN to respond. They have launched a new offensive, a new push, all the way from east of here down to the Mediterranean. It is clear they intend to end this while other nations still contemplate which side of the fence to leap."

"How bad is it?"

"Bad. They have broken through our lines at three points so far, and I don't have to tell you how far our forces are stretched. The war is being fought in every country that's joined the Alliance. We are losing ground at every turn. I know you are recently returned from one mission, but I am afraid I have to send you on another."

"That's what I'm here for."

"Good. I know you have gained some strength recently, and you'll need it. I am sending you to Arras in the north. It is vital our flanks are defended."

Taylor studied the map.

"Arras, that's what, a hundred and fifty klicks from here?" he asked, sounding concerned.

Dupont sighed as he nodded.

"They are almost at the city."

Taylor shook his head.

"What is it, Colonel?"

"Why France? It started here, and it seems no matter where we go and what we do, I always end up back here."

"Yes, I am sorry to say my fair country has become the epicentre of the struggle for the World's freedom."

"When do you want us to leave?"

"Now, time is everything."

Taylor knew what he had to do. He casually saluted, walked out the room, and tapped his comms unit. "Inter-Allied, form up and prepare to move out."

By the time he had gathered his own equipment and got back to the hangar that had become their home, the entire Regiment was formed up with Jones at their forefront. The Rangers' ship was set in the background, and a line of copters in front. Taylor passed Rains. He was airbrushing an American flag onto the side of a well-used copter in French markings.

"See, no matter what, you always find another girl."

"Yeah, thanks," he replied sarcastically.

Taylor stopped before the troops and could see he now commanded over three hundred.

Enough to raise all kinds of hell, he thought.

"Listen up! The UEN is making advances west and covering some serious ground. I have heard, just as all you have, that elements within the US military are heading this way to help us out. That may be true. It may be bullshit. All we know for certain is that to the east the enemy is gaining ground, and General Dupont is deploying us to the northeast to stop them. We are but a few hundred in a war of millions, but let us never forget we have always punched above our weight!"

A cheer rang out.

"In the past, we have fought against Mechs; a faceless and fearsome enemy which none of you would hesitate to put down. Now we fight both Mechs and humans. Some of those humans may be Krys as well, but none of that matters. All you need to know is they are the enemy, and it your job to kill the sons of bitches before they kill you. We've got to win this war, for a far greater one is on the way. Let's do this right. Coordinates and map data have been sent to flight crews, officers, and NCOs. Load up, and good luck to you all!"

Taylor joined Jones who was heading for Rains' copter.

"You know that idea Acosta had for ammunition to take down the aerial drones I told you about?"

"Yes."

"Well, amazingly they work."

"We taking them with us?"

He shook his head.

"Had we been able to wait a day, maybe, but time is not on our side."

"Then I guess we just hope not to meet them."

As he said it, Taylor already knew they would, but fretting over it did no one any good now. Five minutes later, they were lifting off and heading for their new destination. It would be a short journey. After twenty minutes, they felt the copter rock and Rains' voice.

"Incoming fire!"

"I thought they hadn't reached the city yet?" asked Jones.

"That's what I was told!" replied Taylor.

He rushed forward to the cockpit. Missiles were zipping in and out of the craft as they were carried away and ignited by the defence systems of the Rangers' advanced vessel.

"That's a hell of thing!"

"But it can't last, Eddie."

He opened a channel.

"We can't stick this out. Everyone out now, jump, jump, jump!"

Jones ripped open the door and was out before he could even pass on new orders to Rains.

"Put down somewhere safe a few klicks west and look after yourselves!"

Taylor rushed to the door as the last two aboard jumped, and he followed suit. As he hit the open air, he saw a terrifying sight. A swarm of drones were coming for them.

"Oh, shit, no!"

He lifted his shield as he continued to descend, raising his rifle using the targeter on his helmet. A shot bounced from the shield as he did so, and he returned fire with a burst at the nearest target. The last shot he fired clipped the edge of one of the rotors and sent the drone barrelling out of control. He watched it smashed over a shield of one of the troops below him.

As he fired at another target, the swarm passed through them, and he knew they were in trouble. There was nothing the copters or larger vessels could do. As one passed close to Taylor, he swung his rifle out and smashed it hard so that it burst into a dozen pieces. He felt an impact on the backplate of his armour. One of the drones strafed him. Another shot hit one of the thrusters on his legs, and he started to plummet to the ground.

Taylor looked down. He was approaching the roof of a three-storey building at a speed he probably couldn't survive. Just when he thought he was done for, he felt an impact; Jones had got a hold of his side. It slowed their descent a little, but it wasn't enough.

"Oh shit!" was all Taylor had time to scream.

The two of them struck the rooftop and burst through it with little resistance, striking the floor below, through that and the next one down again. They then hit water with a thunderous splash. Taylor just about felt his back knock into the bed of water before coming to the surface and gasping for air. He looked around and saw they had landed in a swimming baths.

"Jones!"

The Captain surfaced a few metres from him and looked around, surprised as he was. Taylor began laughing at the ridiculousness of the situation, and Jones could not help but join in, both realising how lucky they were to be alive.

"What are the odds?" asked Taylor.

"Luck just seems to follow you, you crazy bastard!"

They were clambering out of the pool when Silva rushed in through a side door with Acosta close beside him. They looked up at the huge hole in the ceiling and then at the pool. They were speechless.

"What, never seen a wet marine?" Taylor laughed.

Silva at least managed a smile as they rushed out onto the street and found a few dozen of their unit dug in.

"What's our situation?"

As Taylor said it, a column of drones flew into the street. Everyone in sight opened fire. Their targets were at least easier to track when they had little room to manoeuvre in the narrow gaps between buildings.

"Fuckers," muttered Taylor. He raised his rifle and fired a burst into one of the drones until it crashed through a window of a nearby building. As the rest carried on taking the targets down, he turned to Silva.

"We're scattered across town," replied Silva.

"Any sign of the local forces?"

"There's fighting to the east, certainly. I'd say they're cut off, or they'd be running this way right about now."

"All units advance east, sweep and clear!" he called down the comm.

Taylor led the way and took a bend to a quiet street that seemed untouched by the fighting. He crossed on over to a narrow alley which led on to the parallel street. There he found a dozen French soldiers retreating towards them. They initially raised their weapons to fire but recognised them as friendly. Taylor grabbed one who had Corporal's stripes.

"What's the situation up there?"

"Lost," the man replied faintly.

Taylor could see the hopeless expression in his eyes. They were covered in dirt, and he had blood on him that clearly wasn't his.

"You still got people fighting out there?"

The Corporal nodded. Taylor wiped away grime on his uniform and saw a name tag that read Roux.

"Then what are you doing running this way, Corporal Roux? Your comrades need you."

"We can't stop them. We can't fight them. It's over."

"It's not over. You know why?"

The man shook his head.

"Because I am Colonel Mitch Taylor of the Immortals, and I say it ain't over, you got me?"

The Corporal's eyes flared up a little on hearing the name. He saw the nametag and rank on Taylor, which confirmed it.

"You're here? Here to fight with us?" he asked, perking up.

"That's right. I always was, and I always will be. Now you got some boys who need some help out there, and we're gonna give it to them together, aren't we?"

He turned back to the others with him. "You heard him. We've got the Immortals with us. Nothing can stop us now."

"Then lead on!" Taylor ordered.

He carried on at the front with the Corporal, whose platoon was now mixed with the ragtag group of Inter-Allied Taylor had landed with. It was far from the 'cavalry coming to the rescue' scenario he had been expecting, but the only move was to continue onwards. The gunfire was getting louder, and he knew they were in the right place. Explosions ignited as big guns pounded the area. He wondered where the air support was. As he did, he heard an explosion above and saw a fighter burst into flames; a surface-to-air device knocked it out of the sky.

Ground warfare. It has come down to this once again.

Taylor never liked his time in space, but he at least appreciated the fact that any fighting they did up there was kept away from Earth soil. He longed for that once again. They passed across another street and heard a loud voice.

"Hold it right there!"

They couldn't tell where it had come from and immediately went to ground.

"Identify yourselves!"

"Colonel Taylor, Inter-Allied!"

"Yeah right, who are you really?"

Taylor lowered his weapon and got up."

"What are you doing?" Silva shouted.

He ignored the Sergeant Major and strode forward as if without a concern in the world.

"I am Colonel Taylor, and I am here to save your asses!" he responded defiantly.

Suddenly a head popped up from between the debris of a building, and two soldiers stepped out.

"No, can't be."

"What, you thought we were just a myth?"

Before they could answer him a shell landed on the building above.

"Cover!"

They went to ground as chunks of concrete landed all around. He got up and spat out the concrete dust he had become so familiar with in urban combat.

"Yes, it's me. I'm here. Now what can we do to help?"

He could not see rank on either of the French soldiers, and they looked utterly baffled to be asked such a thing by an officer.

"We are rear guard to Captain Anders. She's dug in two blocks ahead. They're giving us hell, Sir. I don't know how long we can hold."

"Don't you worry; you stay put, and if you see any more of our unit, you send them my way, okay? We got scattered on the drop."

"Yes, Sir."

They carried on past the two soldiers who still looked just as baffled as when they first arrived.

"Think it's wise throwing your name about so much?" asked Jones.

"Why?"

"You're a big target."

"That ain't gonna change, and I'm not hiding from any bastard who wants to kill me."

Jones respected that and did not push the matter. They came through a clearing and found a line of buildings that had been gutted by artillery and were now being used for cover by a line of troops. They were clearly the frontline.

"Who's in charge here?" Taylor shouted.

A female officer beckoned for him to cross the road and join him.

"Captain Anders, I presume?"

"Yes, about time you got here. We need support, and we needed it hours ago. How many are you?"

She appeared to have no regard for his rank, and that

tickled him a little.

"About three hundred."

"Three hundred? Christ, we need thousands not hundreds. We need an army!"

"Yeah, well, you got me. What's your situation?"

"Situation sucks. North is holding at the old defences and should do for some time, but the centre here is under increasing pressure, and half a klick to the south isn't going to hold for much longer."

"What are you facing?"

"Armour, infantry, Mechs. About the only thing we are safe from is the air because anything that comes across the city gets blown out the sky from one side or the other."

"And combat drones?"

"Yes, those too. We were hit by a wave just twenty minutes ago, but they peeled off west."

"That was our welcoming party."

"Then I am sorry, but we could do little to stop them."

"We're working on that."

"Well, I hope you work faster, or neither of us may live long enough to see the results."

They heard the noise of steps and turned to see dozens of Taylor's troops pour into the street.

Thank Christ for that, he thought.

"We'll head a little south and bolster the defences there. I don't know if we're getting much more support if any, Captain, but we have to hold."

"Those are just words, Colonel. We'll give everything we can to hold here, but if it cannot be done, it cannot be done."

"Don't ever say that, Captain!" he shouted for all to hear. "When a fighter says something cannot be done, they only set themselves up to fail. It can be done, and will be done, you got that?"

She looked sheepish but responded loudly, "Yes, Sir!"

Taylor carried on running down the line of crippled buildings. Medics carried the wounded out between the rubble as they passed. It was all too familiar for Taylor. The scene along the lines was the same until they reached the point at which Anders had said was hit the worst. They passed a crater where the bodies of six soldiers lay, and nobody had been able to move as they dealt with the wounded. An ambulance lay crashed and burned in the side of a nearby building, and mechanical mules carried out some of the wounded.

"This ain't good," he muttered to himself. It was the understatement of the century, and Jones had heard it, too.

"Look at them. They can't stick this out for long," he replied.

"We need to take up the slack fast, or they'll falter."

He rushed in to the nearest hole looking out across the battlefield. From there he could see a line of Mechs advancing and firing as they did. He didn't voice a single command to his unit; they all knew what to do. He took careful aim and double tapped one of the Mechs through its faceplate. It died instantly, but three of its comrades quickly returned fire his way, forcing him to duck back down as the shots rushed through the gaping hole and struck the road behind him.

Taylor peered around the corner and could see the burning wrecks of enemy vehicles that had been taken out, and as many Mech bodies as there were humans they fought beside. Even as he admired the hard work their allies had done, a new column of armoured vehicles was arriving.

"Where are they getting all this armour?" Jones asked.

"Most of the stuff left over after the last war wasn't in France, was it?"

Jones sighed. "Well, that's just great!" he replied and fired a few more shots before ducking back.

"Any ideas on our losses from the drones?"

Jones shook his head. "Whatever they are, it could have been a lot worse."

Worse?

It was initially hard to fathom, but then he thought back to how many situations they had been through where the death around them had been a constant week after week.

"RATs! Deploy the RATs!"

The armoured column head across the ground, smashing their way through wrecks and having to drive over the bodies of many who had fallen. The guns fired on the move and pounded their positions as most of the defenders took cover. The first RAT launcher fired and bounced as its target turned and glanced the shot off its hull.

"Fuck, fuck, take them out!" yelled Taylor.

The second fired, and the same tank was blown apart. Cheers rang out across the line as a volley of the launchers fired and another four vehicles were knocked out, and the rest began to fall back.

"We held? We held!" Silva shouted.

It was a surprise to Taylor as well, and he got up to survey the scene. The enemy casualties were horrific, but he looked back to the obliterated street they had fought from, seeing just how few defenders remained. There were only a handful of casualties from Inter-Allied. They now had more in number than the Regiment initially deployed to defend the city. He looked around for his closest friends and found Parker attending to a casualty.

"That was good timing," stated Jones.

"My timing is always impeccable, is it not? Stay put and do what you can to get the wounded out of here," he added.

Taylor retraced his steps to Anders. She was lying sprawled out against a pile of debris. For a moment, he thought she was wounded, but she turned to face him as he approached. She looked exhausted, both physically and mentally.

"I don't know how much more of this I can take," she whispered as he grew nearer.

"You'll do just fine. Are you in charge here?"

She nodded. "Nobody else left for the job. Only officers who aren't dead, wounded, or missing is the Lieutenant over there and myself."

"You've done a hell of a job to keep it together."

He could tell it meant a lot to her, but she tried to pretend it didn't.

Before he could carry on, he looked down at a small light flashing on the display of the Mappad on his arm. It was an incoming call. He quickly tapped to answer and found Dupont before him once again.

"Taylor, how are things there?"

"Bad."

"They are all over. At least you haven't given any ground. The south is faring much worse. Can you redeploy to assist down there?"

"I don't think so, Sir. Not much left to defend this city, bar a few stragglers. Without us, it won't hold."

"That's not the kind of news I need."

"Tell me about it."

"Can anyone else hear this?"

"Affirmative."

He got the message and walked over to a quiet spot.

"You can talk freely now, Sir."

"The honest truth, Taylor, is that we are in trouble. Big trouble. We're stretched thin, and the UEN just keep hitting us. The Mechs are what are making the difference. They're advancing and taking ground without any fear. Their losses are high. We keep knocking 'em down, but more come right back at us."

"Well aware of that, Sir," he replied, thinking it was strange it even needed saying, considering he was on the frontline and witnessing it with his own eyes.

"What do you want me to do?"

"Stay put, do what you're doing. I'll see what I can do in the south."

The communication cut off, and he strolled back to the Captain.

"Something wrong?" she asked.

"Nothing you don't already know. Keep your chin up, Captain. Think like a winner."

He carried on back to Jones. Most of the casualties were gone or being moved as he approached. Taylor slumped down beside him and reloaded his rifle.

"Any news?"

"Nothing good, Charlie."

"Well, what is it?"

"South is taking a beating. Dupont wanted us to head down there and help."

"We can't leave here. It'll fall before we even get to the south."

"That's what I told him."

Jones shook his head, and as he so frequently did when there was a lull in the fighting, drew out his small stove to brew up. Taylor couldn't help but laugh; as he was reminded of the last time he had seen Grey do the same.

"What's so funny?"

"Ah, nothing, nice to see some things never change."

Jones carried on making his brew when Taylor finally asked what he'd been meaning to for a while.

"Any news on Dubois?"

He nodded. "She's gonna make it, but she won't be joining the fight anytime soon."

"Good, she's been through enough."

"Haven't we all?"

As he watched Jones prepare his tea in his ritualistic fashion, they suddenly became aware how quiet the scene was. Gone were the sound of tracked vehicles, of explosions and screaming wounded. There was barely a sound left. Every single boot step could be heard for thirty metres around, and despite being in the middle of a warzone, Taylor felt calm and relaxed, even peaceful.

"Strange isn't it?" he asked.

"What's that?"

"How quiet it is out there."

"Yes, but don't get too used to it. It won't last."

He was right. There seemed little hope of holding the UEN back. Now all he could hope was that his appeal to the World's population would make a difference.

CHAPTER EIGHT

"Incoming!"

A huge pulse of light soared through the sky and struck a building no more than twenty metres along from Taylor. It burst through and struck the road behind. Screams rang out, and as he looked up, he could see a few walking wounded stumbling around. He saw five dead in the crater that was left. They were just like the pulse artillery they saw the Mech armies use. Jones looked as horrified as he did when another two pulses smashed into their positions.

"Take cover!"

He jumped into the corner of the building he had been using as a firing position and huddled into a corner with Jones as low down in the structure as they could get. They knew all they could do now was hope for the best. The ground shook all around them, and they counted several dozen impacts smash their position. Finally it was over.

"Look!" someone cried excitedly.

Taylor couldn't believe anything good could be in sight, but he got up anyway. Hundreds of craft were soaring through the sky, but they were not coming from the east.

"Those aren't UEN," Jones said, standing up beside Taylor.

Mitch lifted his rifle and zoomed in the scope for a better look.

"My God, they're British."

Jones had to see for himself.

"Can't be!"

"It better be," replied Taylor.

A wave of ground attack craft smashed the enemy positions a few clicks east, and they could just make out troops dropping into the fight after them. A dozen craft came their way and put down out in the open plain of crippled vehicles and dead troops.

"Everyone stay put!"

Several of them looked at him puzzled.

"I want to know their intentions before anyone breaks cover!"

Five troops came out of one of the copters. An officer stood between and walked confidently towards Taylor's line. It was Commander Phillips.

"Colonel Taylor!" he called.

"Yeah! What's the deal here, Sir?"

"We just joined this war. We're in this together!"

Taylor couldn't believe his luck. He'd wanted it to be true from the moment he saw the aircraft but had become wary of getting his hopes up. He stepped out from the hole in the building to greet the Commander.

"You look like hell," said Phillips.

"I'm used to it."

"I'm sorry we couldn't come in on this sooner, Colonel, but we're here now."

Jones stepped out to join them, and Phillips looked astonished.

"Well, I'll be. You came back to us? What on Earth did Taylor have to promise you to get you back in the fight?"

"It doesn't matter," he replied, "but I am back for good."

"So what now, Sir? Whose command are we under?"

"Honestly, I don't know. The United States still will not accept your position in this whole damn thing. The British elements of your unit had to go AWOL, just as you did, but I've made sure everyone who matters has turned a blind eye to that. Far as I can tell, you're an independent Regiment under the guidance of General Dupont."

The two of them were as much stunned, as they were pleased.

"Anyway," Phillips carried on, "the British Third Army is tasked with retaking the elements of Northern France under occupation. I am en route to meet with General Dupont to liaise with him in person, if you would like to join me, your whole Regiment that is. You've done enough for now. Let our boys shoulder some of the hard work."

"Gladly, but Captain Anders here has had it far worse. I request they get immediate assistance and relief."

"I'll sort it on the way and see you shortly, Gentlemen," he said, paced back aboard his copter, and it lifted off.

Taylor looked over to Anders, and rather than looking relieved she was in utter shock, having gotten a few moments of peace to reflect on the devastation.

"The fight if over for you, Captain. You did a damn fine job."

"With these losses? How can it be a fine job to have to return home with so few?"

He knew the feeling, and there was no way to make it hurt any less, so he left her to be alone with her thoughts.

"Good luck, Captain."

He hit his comms unit.

"Inter-Allied is moving out. Get the birds here ASAP."

He never thought he'd give the order. Only a half hour ago they were locked in a desperate stand to hold the city.

"With the British in the war, it'll make a hell of a difference," said Jones.

"It will, but not enough, I fear."

"You know we haven't had orders to return to Meaux?"

"Whether we have or not, we're going."

Acosta was pacing up to ask a question when blood suddenly spewed out of his neck and over Taylor's face.

A gunshot echo followed soon after, and Acosta dropped into his arms.

"Sniper!" Jones bellowed.

Taylor hauled Acosta over into the cover of the ruined building beside them and could see he was suffocating as blood gushed out. Mitch put pressure down on his neck, but the blood seemed to spill out through every gap in his fingers.

"Stay with me, Private. Stay with me!"

He coughed and spluttered. Finally, he went limp.

Taylor went white in shock, looking at the fallen marine who had barely even reached manhood. His shock turned to rage, and he wiped some of the blood off his trousers and picked up his rifle and shield.

"That bullet was coming for you," said Jones.

"I don't care!"

"Well you should!"

"I'm gonna get that son of a bitch!"

"That shot came from a klick south away, easy. That's a lot of ground to cover."

"Come with me or don't, but I won't let that fucker live."

Taylor rushed out from cover with his shield held before him and darted over the road to cross over to the next street. A bullet struck the ground just a metre from him as he did so. Jones knew he couldn't let Taylor go alone and rushed on after him.

"Everyone stay put!" he ordered as he rushed after the Colonel.

A shot struck his shield as he covered the open ground. After he got to the other side of the road, he could see Taylor had kept on running without any caution at all.

"Goddamn it, Mitch," he muttered.

He barely saw a glimmer of movement up ahead and chased on after him. He got to a corner and could see nothing at all, but he had no choice but to continue on. He ran on for a full five minutes when he felt an arm grab him by the shoulder and pull him aside. A bullet ricocheted off the wall where his head had been. He breathed a sigh of relief to see it was Taylor.

"This guy is good," said Jones.

Taylor nodded.

"He's come for you, you know that, right? Acosta took that bullet for you."

" I know," he replied, sadly.

"Seems everyone wants a piece of you these days."

"That's nothing new."

"But where did this come from? That video you put out must have really made someone mad."

"They're starting to realise I'm gonna tear the UEN down, if I have to do it with my bare hands."

"So how do you want to play this?"

"Far as I can tell, the shooter is on the ground floor in an apartment building at the end of the street. It runs down our side here."

"Ground floor?"

"I don't know why, but he must be. He's firing on a completely flat trajectory. Trouble is, there ain't no cover getting across the street to him, and it's a long way round."

"Rush him?"

"No, that's a high power rifle. Our shields will only take a few shots from that thing." He point to the buckling of Jones' where it had been struck.

"Shit," he replied.

Taylor pulled out his only smoke grenade from his webbing.

"Smoke the street."

He pulled out a flashbang.

"Then we flash, in case he's got thermal equipment. Then we rush and hope for the best."

"Sounds like a plan."

Taylor ignited the smoke and launched it out into the open street, and Jones did the same. They waited twenty seconds for it to spread and fill the area, and then Taylor launched a flash out into the smoke as far towards the building as he could. He knew the smoke would reduce the effect of the flash, but he had to hope it would be enough to a sniper looking through a scope.

The flash popped, and the sniper recoiled, his eyes burning, and he pulled the trigger. The shot went high, and Taylor knew they were in business. He rushed out from cover and sprinted across the street. Jones could barely keep up and watched his silhouette through the smoke. Taylor launched himself through the window where the sniper had been.

He crashed into the apartment like an elephant and rolled into the furniture, smashing everything in his way. He was on his feet in no time and could see the sniper trying to heave around the huge rifle to fire at him, but it wasn't quick enough. Taylor leapt at him, barging the man with his shield. The sniper hit the wall and bounced off. As he did, Taylor brought up his knee full power into the man's head. He was instantly knocked out cold.

Jones arrived just in time to see Taylor dragging him back out through the wall feet first.

"Human?"

"I wouldn't bet on it, Charlie."

"I just expected, you know, a Mech."

"A Mech sniper sent to kill me? No. They needed a man for this job, and I'm willing to bet any money, he'll ping going through our scanners."

Taylor dragged him the full klick back to the Regiment where the others were boarding the copters. He could see two of them carrying Acosta's body, along with more than ten other casualties they had taken in the bombardment.

"You got the bastard," Silva said. He was overseeing the boarding.

"Damn right."

Silva looked at him more carefully.

"I thought you would have killed him."

"No, no. He's gonna suffer much worse in time, but I want info out of this son of a bitch before then."

Taylor dragged the sniper aboard Rains' copter. He looked less than impressed.

"He even human?" asked Rains.

"No way."

They were in the air moments later, and Jones could see the despair in Taylor's face. They had lost many friends over the years, but somehow, the loss of his youngest marine hit harder than most.

"Hell of a marine he was," said Jones.

"Damn right," replied Taylor.

Landing in Meaux, they could see it was a hive of activity, though so much of the movement was medical vehicles, personnel, and those wounded coming and going. Taylor stepped off the craft, and he turned back to Jones, handing out his orders as he walked away.

"Get them re-equipped and ready to go again within the hour, and see if Reiter has got those web rounds yet."

"Ready? No chance," replied Jones.

"Just do it!" Taylor snapped and continued on.

He was obviously taking Acosta's death hard, and the success of the web rounds would keep his memory alive.

He stepped into Dupont's war room with Acosta's blood still splashed over his filthy armour, but despite several other officers taking offence at his attire, Dupont himself didn't even seem to notice.

"Taylor, good work in the north. You shored up that flank just when we needed it. As you know, the British have finally come in on this war," he said, pointing to Phillips.

"Took you some time to catch up after I left you," said the Commander.

Taylor sighed. "Sniper tried to take me out."

"You personally?" asked Dupont.

"I believe so. Took out of one of my boys instead. This is his blood."

"I'm sorry to hear that," Phillips replied.

"This sniper, did you talk to him?"

Taylor shook his head. "Not yet, but he's alive."

"A Krys agent?"

"Must be, General."

"Only a matter of time till you got targeted, I guess," Phillips added.

"What are my orders?"

Dupont looked confused.

"You've done enough for now, Colonel. Find out more about this sniper and have your people enjoy a respite."

"Rest? General we were in combat for one day. We are ready to go back in."

"It's okay, Mitch," said Phillips. "We'll need you soon enough."

He knew he wasn't getting anywhere and turned and left. They were right about one thing, the sniper. Many questions still rolled around his mind about the incident, and he wanted information as much as he wanted payback. He went on through B13 to the cellblock, past Jones' clone, and onto the next cell. Taylor stepped inside the first doorway leading to the observation room and found Rossi there with a datapad.

"Hello, Doctor."

She jumped at the sound of his voice. She turned to speak and then looked at the dried blood on his clothing.

"Are you all right, Colonel?"

"Just fine. That bastard in there caused this blood, but it ain't mine."

"I am sorry to hear that, Colonel."

He nodded in gratitude. "Please, stop calling me Colonel. You are a civilian. Call me Mitch."

"Oh…okay."

"Then tell me about this Krys scumbag. What have you learnt?"

She looked confused.

"What is it?"

"This man is not a Krys agent. He is not a clone."

"What? He must be."

"Sorry, Colonel, but as far as I can tell, he is every bit as human as we are."

Taylor looked into the cell and studied the man more

closely. He was confused by Rossi's findings.

"This man was sent to kill me personally. Are you telling me he knew who I was, lived through the last few wars, and yet still came after me?"

She shrugged. "I don't know what to tell you, Colonel."

"Mitch."

"Mitch. As far as we can tell, he is human."

"And have you asked him why he came after me?"

"I am a scientist, not an interrogator."

"Then it's time for me to ask him some questions."

"I wouldn't go in there, Colonel. You are not thinking clearly and have obviously experienced some significant trauma. You should leave this to someone less… affected by his actions."

"Dupont has asked me to find out more about this guy, and that is precisely what I intend to do."

"Just remember that he is human, whether you like it or not. He is not a clone, not an alien."

"I don't give a damn what he is. He's gonna talk."

Taylor ripped open the door and stepped inside. The sniper has been stripped to his vest and pants and had his wounds cleaned up. He recognised Taylor instantly and showed just a little fear in his eyes.

"I am Colonel Mitch Taylor of the Inter-Allied Regiment, but you already knew that, didn't you?" he said, taking a seat. "And don't give me any of that name, rank, serial number shit. I'm not interested. I want to know why you did it. Why you would come after me?"

He spoke without hesitation.

"Because you are an enemy to this world. A barrier to progression and peace."

Taylor shook his head.

"What the fuck are you talking about? I've been fighting for peace from day one. I want to defend this earth from invaders. What about you?"

"The Krys bring with them science and medicine like we have never known. They only want to live on this world beside humanity."

"Well, they got a funny way of showing it. They didn't exactly show passports on arrival and fill out visas. You can't really believe the shit that is coming out of your mouth?"

He remained silent.

Taylor was growing tired of him already. He leapt forward and grabbed the man by his vest top and punched him on the jaw.

"Now tell me the real truth, why did you come after me?"

"Because you are an enemy of all that is good in the World. You would have us fight until no man, woman, or child still lives."

Taylor hit him again.

"I don't believe you. Why did you come to kill me?"

Taylor hit him once more, and as he did so, the door

flung open beside him. Jones rushed in and pulled him off the prisoner.

"Mitch, what the hell are you doing?"

"Get the hell off me!" he screamed, shrugging Jones off, but he grabbed him again and pulled him out of the cell back to where Rossi was still standing. She looked at him in a new light as if she were afraid. Jones shut the door behind them so the three of them were alone.

"What in high hell is going on here?" asked Jones.

He got no answer, so turned to Rossi for one.

"The subject in that room is human, and yet the Colonel believes him to be a clone."

Jones was as surprised as Taylor had been and was starting to understand why he had lost it.

"Human?"

"There are plenty of bad people in the World, or people with conflicting opinions to our own. There always were. Why would you assume every enemy has to be alien?"

"She's right, you know," added Jones. "The whole of the UEN can't all be clones and Mechs. There must be millions of people who have bought into their way of thinking. They probably feel just as strongly as we do."

"So what are we supposed to be trying to understand, the feelings of the aliens and their enablers now?"

"Maybe you should, Colonel. You might learn something," said Rossi. "The question we really should be asking is, do people like the subject in their support of the

UEN and alien philosophies, or have they been lied to as to the deal they're getting?"

"Why does it matter?" Taylor spat back.

"It matters a lot. If they have been lied to and are fighting under false pretences, there is hope of winning them back yet."

Taylor righted himself and calmed down, accepting she was talking sense.

"I always assumed they were lied to in order to fight us, why would they do so otherwise?"

"I wouldn't like to speculate," replied Rossi. "But I think we should leave it to trained investigators and interrogators to work with this subject and get a better understanding of what we face."

It was an odd concept to Taylor. He'd only ever seen their situation as black and white, human and alien. To him every one who fought against them was an alien or no better than one.

"This is worse than I thought," he muttered. "How can we get these people to see sense?"

"We may never do so."

"So what, we just have to fight them till death or surrender?"

"Same as any war," said Jones.

Taylor had somehow held on to the belief that the humans fighting for the UEN could be 'converted' and would come on board.

"That bastard killed Acosta and tried to kill me. I want him to pay."

"But would you not do the same to the enemy?" asked Rossi. "He didn't kill civilians. He didn't slit your friend's throat in the night. He fired on you in a war zone, as you were doing to his comrades."

Taylor knew it was true, but he didn't like hearing it.

"This was a hell of a lot easier when we only fought aliens."

"This is why they are doing what they are doing,' said Jones. "They're screwing with our heads and weakening the whole of humanity in the process."

Taylor had seen and heard enough. He turned to leave. Jones reached to grab his arm and pleaded, "Mitch, just wait a minute," but he shrugged it off and went through the door. He stepped out of the prison block, not knowing what to do or where to go. His faith in humanity had been shattered in one single encounter. He needed air and stepped outside the complex, but even as he did so his comms unit flashed, and a message came through.

"Colonel Taylor, report to General Dupont immediately."

He was initially annoyed to have been bothered during a moment of peace, but he then felt more than anything else he needed something to take his mind to a better place. He needed a job to do, a mission to undertake. He strode on quickly to Dupont's war room, stepped inside, and found a serious tone overshadowed everyone gathered there. They were frantically in conversation, but Taylor could not make out the subject.

Phillips approached and his face was grim.

"What the hell's going on?" asked Taylor.

"UEN has gotten control over the Earth Defence Grid and are threatening to turn it on all nations in support of the EA."

"What? How did they manage it? Are there not safe measures in place to stop it being turned on Earth?"

"Yes, nobody knows how they got control of them, but they did, and they have two dozen war ships defending the grid. No way we can get near them without them opening fire."

"So what is happening here?"

"We're trying to come to some kind of solution, or any sensible idea really as to how we can stop them."

"Anyone got any good ideas yet?"

Phillips shook his head. "Full on assault is the only thing so far which makes any sense, but I can't see how it can work before half the capitol cities in the EA are vaporised, including London, now we have joined the fight."

"You sure chose a peachy time to get involved."

"What is the US saying?"

"Nothing yet. We're waiting to hear their response."

"Colonel Taylor!" yelled the General.

The room was silenced.

"I see Commander Phillips has explained the situation to you, got any ideas?"

Taylor seemed surprised.

"Come on, Taylor. You've successfully completed some of the most outrageous and far-fetched missions known in any of our lifetimes. Don't be so modest. We need to stop this defence grid. How would you do it?"

The entire room was looking to him, and when he knew they were relying on him to come up with an answer to save millions of lives, he hesitated."

"Go on, Taylor. This is right up your street," whispered Phillips.

"General, seems to me the avenue of negotiation is closed to us. All that remains is action. I propose a direct assault on the defence grid to retake control of the weapons and ensure the safety of us all."

His comment was met by heckles from other officers in the room.

"Let him speak!" Dupont ordered.

The room was silenced.

"Please, Colonel, enlighten us as to how you would achieve this, considering they are so heavily guarded and ready to fire within just a few minutes notice?"

"I would send an EMP up."

"That would knock out everything up there, anything we had also, and the enemy vessels would be operational again before we could get there in any number," Phillips replied.

"Nothing big, no, but a few small fast ships could pass through at speed undetected. Nothing more than maybe three to five craft. They'll have to bypass visual identification or risk bringing in a wave of support. Yes, we need the EMP to appear as an accident, a malfunction of a nearby satellite. Make it appear as if we lose everything too and do not know the grid is down. We play dumb while a select few are doing the job."

"And the German's latest battleship, it has shielding from EMPs. Even its primary systems recover from EMPs in sixty seconds."

"Okay, so we set a diversion also. It's all doable."

"And you would be the leader of such a mission?" Dupont asked.

"I would gladly do so."

"Mmm, I know that you would, but I am not sure all our allies would agree," he said, pointing to a US officer sitting at the table he had not previously noticed. Taylor did not recognise the woman but knew she would not be a fan of his.

She opened her mouth to speak, and he expected to hate anything that came out of it.

"Colonel Taylor may be a hero of the EA, but he is a traitor to the United States. He cannot, and will not, be trusted to carry out a mission so vital to the security of our nations."

Everybody was silenced and turned to him for his response. He could feel the anger brewing inside his very soul, but he would not let it destroy him.

"Where was the United States when the UEN freed Mechs and gave them weapons? Where was the United States when France was invaded? I will not be lectured by an office clerk with an attitude problem. The US always should have been in this fight. I knew that from the beginning. That it has now joined only confirms I was right, and if you want to be so petty as to drag me down just to save face, shame on you."

Everyone in the room looked to the US officer in disgust. They all secretly felt just the same. She was blushing and flustered, and did not know how to respond. She shrunk into her chair as if she wanted to find a hole and jump in it.

"You see, I am the blunt instrument needed in war, and as much as you don't like me at times, I am a necessary pain in the ass. I'll do this mission for you all because I can, because I will, and because you won't find a better team for the job. When you accept that, you call me."

With that, he turned and left. Phillips could not help but smile. Taylor walked right out and didn't stop until he reached the hangar that was the new home of the Regiment. They were lying about with many taking a nap in the afternoon heat. Parker was the first one to notice him and acknowledge his arrival.

"Colonel is back in the house!" she yelled.

"So what's next for us?" asked Silva. "Take on the World single-handedly?"

Many of them laughed, but Taylor raised his hand to quieten them down.

"You laugh, but it isn't so far from the truth!"

Suddenly all attention was turned on him.

"Something big has come up, and I volunteered myself along with anyone willing to come along for the ride. I can't give you details just yet, but what I can say is I expect General Dupont to accept my offer within the hour!"

They shouted in excitement even though they had no idea what they were getting themselves into, but they trusted Taylor no matter what. Jones stepped up to his side and was clearly concerned after seeing him with the prisoner earlier on. He took him by the shoulder and moved him a few steps out of sight from the rest of the unit.

"Sure this is a good idea, Mitch? You've been a little... wired recently."

"So my faith in humanity has been rocked a little, what's the issue?"

"That maybe taking God knows how many of us on a suicide mission when you aren't a hundred percent isn't smart?"

"Oh, come on. If you wanted me at a hundred percent, you should have come to me before the first invasion."

Parker appeared at his side and took his arm to lead him away. She gave him a glass that looked like it was filled with beer, but as he drank it was hit by fizz and a lack of alcohol.

"You okay, Mitch?"

"Yeah, why does everyone keep fucking asking?"

"You know you've been through a lot."

"Oh, don't give me this shit, nothing has changed here. Shit is the same as it always has been. I haven't changed a single bit."

"All right, okay. I just don't want you biting off more than you can chew."

Taylor shook his head in disbelief.

"Don't you lose faith in me, not now, not after all we have been through."

"I just don't want to see you get hurt."

"Then believe in me, like you always used to."

He looked into her eyes and could see there was still doubt deep down.

"Please, if we're gonna make it through any of this, I need to know you have my back every step of the way."

She nodded in agreement, and he could see her expression change.

"Okay, I will," she said sincerely.

He took a step back and looked at her carefully, seeing she truly meant it. He knew he had lost his stride with the sniper incident, and it was time to get back on track.

"Seriously, the whole World is in trouble. They need us at our very peak, the best we can be. We need to set aside all other shit in our lives and be what we are famous for. We are the Immortals, and that is what the World needs right now."

She accepted all that he had said, and they sat down to enjoy whatever non-alcoholic drink she had given him. But their peaceful time didn't last long. Just twenty minutes after laying down to rest, Dupont arrived at the hangar with a number of his staff.

"Taylor!"

The room fell silent. Mitch got up; noting the obnoxious American officer who had tried to destroy him earlier that day accompanied the General.

"Oh, please," he said.

"It's okay, Colonel. I have been in contact with my counterparts in the US, and despite their reservations, they have accepted you are the right man for the job."

Taylor smiled in response and looked past the General to the female officer who tried not to make contact.

"I'll do it…"

"Excellent."

"However! I want an assurance from the US President himself that no charges will be made against myself or any who serve with me."

"For what exactly?" the woman asked.

"Anything, everything," he replied. "No charges of

going AWOL, insubordination, tax evasion, whatever. I want a guarantee that we are safe from prosecution from any shit that might be levied against us. I think we deserve it."

Dupont looked back to the American officer and expected a response. She looked pissed off but finally agreed.

"I want that documented before we leave, and then we're good to go. I need every piece of intel we have on this defence grid. I want an EMP set to go. I want the fastest small transports available on Earth, and I want it all in the next thirty minutes. We have a job to do, a big job, and I want every chance of making it work."

"You've got every resource you need, Colonel. We're on a tight schedule here, and you know what's at stake. Do whatever you need to."

"Then we're in business. Inter-Allied is at your service and good to go!"

CHAPTER NINE

The officers and senior NCOs sat about a briefing room looking at the blue prints of the German battleship, Nassau. There was utter silence as they stared at it and clearly wracked their brains for a solution to the behemoth they were facing. The air was thick, as none of them had even had a moment to wash since returning from their last mission. Taylor wiped the sweat from his brow as he felt the salt on his mouth from where it was seeping down his face. Eventually Silva broke the silence.

"Sure we can't send the fleet against them?"

Taylor nodded. "The EA fleet would have a better than average chance of victory against everything they have, but not quick enough to stop that grid from firing. If those weapons fire on Earth, it's all over. The EA and any allies we still have will be smashed."

"So we have about a thirty-second window to get past

this thing and get to the defence grid before we're blown to shit?" Jones asked.

"Hey, I'm all for saving the planet and all, but this is crazy!" added Rains.

The room was silenced once again and all looked to Taylor.

"Look, I didn't order any of you to be here. I volunteered, and I am not asking any one of you to follow me. That is your choice."

"We want to follow you," said Grey. "We just want to know we're risking our lives with at least a chance of success, and not just being blown out of the sky without a hope in hell."

Taylor nodded. "Most of the ships in the area will be out of action for some time, both ours and theirs, so the Nassau is our primary concern. Thirty seconds of being without power is enough to make her vulnerable."

"You're not thinking what I think you're thinking?"

He nodded. "Yeah, Jones, we have to board her and the defence grid simultaneously."

Silva shook his head. "And with how many men?"

"There are only a handful of ships fast enough to get from beyond the EMP range into action before that thirty seconds is up. I figure we could get maybe a hundred and fifty or so."

"A hundred and fifty to take on a battleship and the defence grid?" asked King. "The Nassau alone probably has a couple of hundred marines aboard."

"Yes, but scattered throughout the vessel and without the combat experience and skills of this Regiment."

"That's a big assumption to make," muttered Jones.

"At this point we are gonna have to make the best of a bad choice of options and go with it. We're leaving within the hour, so we better have a damn good idea of what we're doing," Taylor replied.

They all knew there was little else to be considered.

"Say we can pull this off and stop the defence grid, what happens to us then?" asked Grey.

"We hope the EA fleet can get to us in time to assist and hope for the best. Right now, our main concern must be deactivating those weapons, or it's all over."

They all knew their lives meant nothing compared to the importance of the operation's success. None of them wanted to say it, but they knew it was true.

"Captain King, I want you and your Company on standby for this. If we can succeed in disabling both targets, you will come to our aid, because trust me, we'll need it. Dupont wants me to take on the defence grid personally, so I'll need a volunteer to lead the Nassau element of this operation."

It was a big thing to ask, and he knew who he wanted for the job.

"Nice to know I'm wanted," said Jones. "Yes, I'll do it."

Taylor nodded in appreciation. He still wasn't certain

Jones was quite the man he used to be, but he certainly was still the right soldier for the job.

"Has the US declared war yet?" asked King.

Taylor shook his head.

"As far as I understand it, they recognise the threat the defence grid poses and condemn its use against Earth."

"Well that's a big fucking help."

Taylor grunted. "Well they have at least accepted our position on this and are guaranteeing us all immunity from prosecution for anything they wanted to levy against us should we pull this off."

"And survive," added Silva.

"Then they can at least give us control of the rest of Inter-Allied. Jackson and Ota, two extra Companies could go a long way in aiding King," said Jones.

"I'll see what I can do," he replied, turning his attention to the Nassau diagram.

"This blueprint definitely right?"

"I bloody hope so," replied Jones.

"Commander Phillips says so, and I am inclined to trust his sources," Grey said.

Jones was carefully studying every element of the ship.

"We'll hit them here," he finally stated.

Taylor looked carefully at where he was pointing. It was a power source for the ship's weapon systems buried many decks below the surface. Taylor looked confused.

"Why there? We need a diversion, that's all."

"You need to be sure you are gonna make it, and the only way to be sure of that is if you aren't getting shot at. If I pinpoint everything at my disposal at that point, there is a fair chance we can give you a clear run. Maybe even a chance of giving our fleet a run at taking her out."

"It's suicide," added King. "Being a diversion is one thing, but you start causing that much trouble, and you'll bring a world of shit down on your head."

Jones shrugged. "We have one chance of getting this done, so let's do it right. All that is important is that we stop that weapon system. I think I can provide the best chance of Taylor making it."

Nobody responded while they waited for Taylor's opinion.

"It's a sound plan," he finally responded. "Anyone offer another in the next five minutes?"

"Board the Nassau and turn her guns on the defence platforms?" asked King.

Taylor mulled it over. "Not a bad plan, but there are too many variables. There are all kinds of ways those weapons could be shut down by the crew before we could make use of them, but I like your thinking. The UEN knew I was coming last time, and I bet they'll expect it again. Let's use that."

"UEN obviously wants your head."

"Yeah, Jones, so you want to be a diversion? You play me. From the moment we board, we go in full environmental suits, visors shut. We'll use voice scramblers to mix our two voices. As far as anyone else is concerned you will be me, and you will be going for the Nassau."

The others couldn't believe what they were hearing. Jones had already volunteered for a crazy mission and was having yet more danger thrust upon him.

"I like it," Jones replied.

"All right, not one word of this switch to anyone outside of this room until we're aboard our craft, you got that?"

They all grunted with approval.

"Right then, you know what you have to do, and Jones, you'll be flying with Rains. We have to give every indication that you are the real Taylor."

"Always saw myself as a Colonel someday," he replied with a smile.

* * *

"Ready?" Jones asked, looking at Taylor.

They were standing in Taylor's quarters and now in each other's uniforms.

"Yep, now remember who you're supposed to be, and try and stay in character. Once they know Colonel Taylor is heading for them, they'll do everything they can to end you."

"Not my first rodeo," Jones jested.

"No. The plan is simple. Stick to it and this can work.

Good luck out there." He offered out his hand as a last gesture of friendship before they stepped out publicly. Jones took it gladly.

"You know of all the men and women in the World who could be going up there to do this, it was always going to be us. It always is."

"That is both our honour and our curse, Charlie."

Taylor pulled on the helmet, and Jones did the same. Taylor reached to the controls on the arm of his suit and tapped a few buttons. The visor shut and went to blackout so that his face was covered. Jones did the same.

"Up and at 'em," said Taylor, doing his best to mimic Jones' mannerisms, and the suit modified his accent. Jones shook his head, as it was an eerie thing to hear. They turned and stepped out of the room to find Inter-Allied formed up with helmets on just as Taylor had ordered. Not an ounce of skin could be seen on any of them. Taylor stepped to one side and let Jones go forward to take charge, which he did so with confidence."

"You all know what you have to do. You all know what's at stake! Let's do this right. Load up and move out!"

That was short and sweet, Taylor thought, remembering his rambling speeches at such times. Three ships for each Company were all they had, and he watched as Jones boarded Rains' craft; so few souls. It seemed so insignificant for what they were going to face.

He took his seat to see he was amongst Jones' Company.

They were men and women he had known well, but he had commanded few personally in combat. As the doors shut, he got up to address them.

"Listen up! I am sorry to have kept you all in the dark on this one, but it is the way it had to be."

As he said that, he raised his helmet visor. Several others did the same to get a look at him with their own eyes.

"The Nassau isn't our target. It is Captain's Jones'. You are coming with me to the real target. This secrecy was necessary until now. All communications from and to this vessel are now blocked until we reach our destination. I tell you now because once we're up there I want everyone to know the deal. This message is being relayed to the other two ships via platoon commanders."

Nobody said a word, but all raised their faceplates as he continued.

"All you need to know is that somehow we need to stop the defence grid. Every officer and senior NCO amongst us has access codes that will override the system from the inside, but how we do it really doesn't matter. You got that?"

"Yes, Sir!" they shouted.

Every single fighter under his command was from the British Army, and it brought a smile to his face at how bizarre it felt, and yet how little they cared. He looked around to get his bearings of whom he had with him. So many of the British paras he had come to know well were long gone from this world. He panned around, looking at the nametags on those sitting around him. He recognised almost every single one of them, and yet could rarely connect a face with each name.

Sergeant Herbert stood out to him, a tall but quiet man who had so frequently been close at Jones' side during the worst of it. Taylor couldn't remember speaking more than a dozen words to him in the time they had served together. The other side of the room he could see Corporals Brown and Harris. There were just twenty-five of them aboard.

"Sergeant Herbert will command his own platoon with Brown his second. The rest of you are with me. Remember, as far as you are concerned, I am Captain Jones, and that is how you will address me. If I should fall, it is essential that you keep going forward. You find a way to disable or destroy the defence grid, you hear me?"

"Yes, Sir!"

Dupont better have some serious reinforcements for us, he thought.

They all knew the EMP would mean they'd be waiting some time for help, but they prayed it would be sooner rather than later. Taylor looked down at his watch. Twenty seconds till the EMP. He counted it down in his head, watching the seconds pass. It finally hit zero. He stepped up to the cockpit.

"Did it work?"

"That's affirmative Col…sorry…Captain. Nothing

much left to see."

Taylor looked out to see they were passing out of the atmosphere to complete darkness at a rapid speed.

"Utter blackout up here. Never thought I'd see it in all my days," the pilot replied.

"Yeah, well, let's hope it stays that way for a while."

* * *

Jones was looking out at the same blackness as Taylor and admiring the tranquillity that would be so short lived. He looked back to see Parker sitting in the nearest seat to the cockpit and realised how much Taylor was relying on him. He was leading almost everybody Taylor cared for into a suicidal mission. He had volunteered for it, but he had never asked Taylor to give him command of all those he held so dear.

There was nothing left to say now as they raced towards the silhouette of the Nassau. It was a vast ship that was part battleship and part carrier. There were still no lights visible, but they could see the outlines of a few support vessels floating in space between them.

"Cut all lights, and do whatever you can to avoid detection."

"Already done, boss," Eddie replied.

"Cut engines now, everything."

Rains did so without question, and everything went

silent as they soared through space towards the hulking vessel without any noise at all, until Rains broke the silence.

"Really think this can work?" he whispered, seemingly concerned the whole enemy fleet could be listening in.

"Why wouldn't it?" replied Jones.

"I dunno. Few fools try and take on a fucking battleship, you don't think that's a little crazy?"

"It is ambitious."

Rains chuckled for a moment before the seriousness of his situation silenced him.

"What the hell is that?" asked Jones.

Rains squinted at the space before them. Lights began to appear on the Nassau, and then he saw the light reflect and reveal a small vessel on the path ahead of them. Rains grabbed for the controls to manoeuvre, but he knew they had no power.

"We can't risk it," said Jones.

"We don't put some power down, then we'll be done for anyway."

Jones thought about it for just a few seconds before replying. "All right, but the absolute minimum needed to get clear."

Rains fired the landing boosters to alter their course, but even as he did so, he could see they weren't going to make it.

"This is gonna be rough."

"More power!" Jones shouted.

"Too late! Hold on!"

They slammed into the ship that appeared to be a small frigate without power. The impact rocked them hard, and Jones almost fell to his feet. He tried to hang on to a railing. Jones expected the ship to crumble and break apart any moment, but amazingly they were thrown into a spin.

"What the hell, Rains?" he shouted.

"I'm a pilot not a miracle worker!"

"Get us power!"

"I can't. The engines are shot!"

They were barrelling out of control, and the only relief they had was that they would blend in with all the other craft floating about space.

"Tell me something, Rains!"

"I got no engines. Life support systems are failing."

"Can you get us to the Nassau?"

He looked out to see them approaching rapidly.

"It's not a question of reaching them, but not dying on impact!"

He was frantically trying anything he could to slow them down when he finally managed to fire a few landing thrusters. Jones could see the light they were emitting from the cockpit, but they had larger problems to worry about now.

"We're losing velocity, but not quick enough."

"Any ideas?"

Rains shook his head. "This bird ain't got nothing left

to give!"

"If we jump now, let the ship make impact, and then use our own boosters to reduce velocity and make the breach, would that work?"

Rains mulled it over for just two seconds before finally shrugging. "Maybe, best chance we got at least!"

Jones rushed to the door, hit the emergency release, and ripped it open.

"Everyone follow me. Get your speed down quick and head for the breach!"

He jumped out and just had to hope the others would quickly follow. As he entered space, he could see lights firing up all along the hull of the Nassau, and it was a frightening sight to be in her gun line. He hit his boosters and was relieved to see the instant reduction in velocity, and the other couple of dozen troops joined him. Their ship soared past them. It had recovered from its spin but was still racing for the battleship.

Jones could just make out the shape of Taylor's three craft passing close by the stern of the vessel and knew they were cutting it close. He turned back to their own ship and saw it crash into the side of the battleship. Half of the hull smashed over the thick armour; the rest pierced through and punched a hole several metres wide.

We're in business.

He turned to his side to see Rains join him and give him the thumbs up. The times Rains had ended up with them in shoulder-to-shoulder combat now were beyond counting and getting a little silly. As they got to twenty metres, Jones adjusted his positioning and looked around one last time to try and see the two other ships with him, but they were nowhere to be seen. *We're on our own,* he thought.

Jones tucked in his rifle and shield as close to his body as possible, and they raced for the breach at a speed that was still far faster than he would have liked. He burst through the breach and found the blast doors had already isolated the room. He hit the deck hard and slid twenty metres along the metal flooring, finally crashing into a thick bulkhead and coming to a halt.

He had to hope his suit was fully intact. As he got to his feet, he half expected to come under fire any moment, but it never came. He looked around to see they were inside a fighter maintenance bay, and there was no one to be seen but the twenty-five souls including himself who had breached the hull of the Nassau. Emergency lighting was on, and it was a sign of how quick the ship's systems were recovering. For all the danger they had just jumped into, all Jones could think was, *I hope Taylor made it.*

"We need to get out of this area now!" he ordered.

Rains was already at a small maintenance door fiddling with something, as Parker tried to find a way past the large blast doors which seemed to be the main way out. Within a few seconds, Rains had the door open and prised apart.

"How in the hell did you do that?" asked Herrera.

"You think this is the first time I've had to break out of somewhere?"

"All right, go, go," said Jones.

He looked down at the Mappad on his arm, trying to work out where they were, but he had no real time information, only the static map he had to interpret himself. There were dozens of fighter bays aboard, and he was desperately trying to look for where the room might be that they had landed in. The last of the group were through with just Rains waiting to shut the door behind him.

"Where will this take us?"

Rains shrugged. "No idea, but it's the only way we'll get out without blowing the place to hell."

Jones knew it was the best option too, but he wished he had even some clue as to where they were. He remembered they had entered at the port side of the vessel, but they could be anywhere within a few dozen floors. The line came to a halt as they waited for Jones to reach the front and make a decision. He pushed on past and saw they had reached a crossroads in what was some kind of maintenance shaft only. He didn't even hesitate to carry on over and led them deeper on into the ship.

"Know where you're going?" whispered Rains.

"No better than you do."

"Great," he mumbled.

"You just remember when we get out there that I am Colonel Taylor, and you make it loud and clear for all to hear. Pass it on," replied Jones.

The whisper carried back down the corridor as Jones reached a doorway. He looked back and signalled for Rains to come forward. The Lieutenant pulled a control box from the wall, and after fiddling for thirty seconds, the door finally slid open. They all raised their rifles as they realised they were entering one of the main decks of the ship. It was still on emergency lighting, but as Jones took the first step out, the main lights fired up. He jumped to the opposing wall for cover.

He'd half expected an ambush, but as the lights settled, he could see three German marines at one side, looking confused and staring at them.

"Taylor, get down!" Rains shouted, just as he had been told to.

As the name rang out, the enemy marines began to raise their rifles, but Jones was already firing. The first one was struck down, and the other two jumped for cover.

"Forward!"

Jones pushed his shield out before him and advanced as a gun line, with the others laying down fire. The injured marine was clipped again in the same arm, and his comrade dragged him back.

"Colonel Taylor!" Parker called out.

Jones looked around to see Eli was doing everything

she could to make his name travel the length of the corridor. He looked up and saw a domed camera module in one corner of the corridor. He strode up to it and stood square on in plain view for whoever was watching to see his rank and name tag before raising his rifle and blowing it to bits.

"Think that worked?"

"We can hope, Parker," he replied, looking at his Mappad. Then he noticed a sign on the wall. They were on deck 1H7.

"What the hell does that mean?"

He had the blueprint, but without any indicator as to how the actual floor names related to anything they were looking at.

"Silva, come in," he said through his communicator.

No response came.

"They must be jamming all frequencies. We probably haven't got more than ten metres range on comms."

"Then we're alone," replied Parker.

"Plan stays the same, and we cause as much trouble along the way as we can."

He looked at the Mappad once again, took his best guess at where they might be, and carried on the direction of the marines they had been fighting. They reached the body of the fallen marine, and all Jones could think was why? He looked like them and had probably fought beside them in the last war.

"Why are they fighting us?" he said when he meant to just think it.

Parker grabbed his arm and stopped him for a moment. "You okay?"

He couldn't see her face through the clouded visor, but he could hear the concern in her voice. It all seemed so senseless to him, more so than the wars they had fought through previously, but he knew he had to keep it together.

"Silva will find our target. You can be sure of that," she claimed to reassure him.

It was true. The Sergeant Major wouldn't quit until he was dead. Jones continued on without another word as they made their way deeper into the ship. Barely a minute later, they reached a crew quarters that had just two occupants, desperately trying to pull on their armour. Parker leaned in and shot both of them through the legs.

Jafar passed by and stopped for a moment. He seemed surprised at the sight. For a moment, Jones thought from his body language that he was shocked at the brutality against their own race, but instead he raised his rifle to finish the job.

"No!" screamed Jones.

It was too late. Gunfire tore through the two injured crewmembers. Jafar turned to him and raised the visor off his helmet with a puzzled expression on his face.

"Never leave an enemy combatant still combat effective to any degree," he stated.

Jones knew he was right, but it still didn't feel right. He turned and carried on at the head of the column. They took a bend, and Jones was met with a burst of gunfire ricocheting off his shield. Parker yanked him back into cover.

"Lay down your weapons!" a voice cried.

Jones looked back at Parker.

"Reason with them. Tell them who you are."

Jones had no idea if it would work or for which reason she was suggesting it, but it was worth a shot.

"This is Colonel Taylor of the Inter-Allied Regiment, European Alliance! Right now, the UEN is preparing to fire the Earth defence grid against targets on the ground, military and civilian, that will change the face of this world forever! You must know that is wrong. Join us, or lay down your weapons, and let us pass!"

Silence ensued, and he looked back at Parker for an opinion. "How was that?" Jones was no negotiator, and he felt more than a little uneasy trying to be one while simultaneously acting as Taylor.

"Little straight, but yes, I think it did the job."

He looked to Jafar who only shook his head.

"Folly," the alien simply replied.

They could both see Jafar didn't comprehend what they were trying to accomplish. They could hear a few mumblings from down the corridor, and Taylor's name being bandied around. Jones was hopeful until a voice shouted back, "Colonel Taylor, you are ordered to lay down your weapons and come out with your hands up!"

Jones shook his head. He knew it was too much to ask for. Without another word, he drew a flashbang from his armour, primed it, and launched it down the corridor. Before it had even ignited, he leapt out into the corridor, using his shield to protect him from both the grenade and any gunfire. He sprinted down the corridor at them with Jafar close behind.

As the grenade ignited, he could see the marines were Reitech equipped, with near enough everything he currently carried except for the shield, and it made all the difference. He held it before him, using the helmet targeter to kill one after the other as they scrambled for cover. Shots rushed past him from either side, as others of the platoon flanked the two of them and kept up the pace.

They had covered half the distance when they saw the last three marines throw down their weapons.

"Cease fire!" Jones screamed.

Even Jafar did exactly as ordered. Jones realised that he was utterly loyal. He just didn't understand the concept of letting enemies live.

"What do we do with them?" Parker asked.

"They'll only come back to bite us in the ass," replied Herrera.

Jones paced up to the three marines. They looked terrified, as if they'd never fought a real battle in their lives. He couldn't bring himself to kill them but knew restraining them could lead to them quickly being freed. Imprisonment made him feel sick to the stomach, and he had no idea where they could do it anyway. He pulled off the helmet of the nearest one and then drew out his pistol, reversing it so the grip was forward.

"Either you take the pain, or you let him end you now," he said and pointed to Jafar. The marine looked at the towering alien and then turned back to Jones and nodded in agreement. Jones smacked him across the head with his pistol, knocking him unconscious immediately. Parker and Herrera did the same for the other two. They knew it risked serious injury, but it was better than execution.

Jones carried on until he suddenly stopped at a radiation warning sign. He looked down at his Mappad and smiled when he could see where they were.

"We're not far now."

As he said it, they heard all the systems in the ship power up.

Shit, thought Jones.

"Let's move!"

He rushed onwards, knowing their presence and location would be common knowledge, and the camera recordings from when they first boarded would soon be relayed to the bridge.

Once they think Taylor is aboard, all hell is going to break loose.

As they took a bend up ahead, they were met with

gunfire from half a dozen marines dug in where they were heading. Jones didn't even flinch when the first shots hit his shield, and he kept up the pace towards them.

Thank God they haven't got shields.

The weight of gunfire was too much for his, and it buckled over his arm. He knew it could only take another shot or two and it was done for. He increased to a sprinting pace and rushed at the defenders. They looked terrified by their unflinching aggression.

With one swing, Jones' shield passed over a support joist a marine was using for cover. He smashed the edge of his shield into the man's head, snapping his neck with the impact. It sent Jones into a spin. As he recovered, he fired a burst into one of the other's faces, just as Jafar and Parker reached his position still firing. Jones drew out his Assegai and turned to face another, but was too late. An Assegai of one of the enemy marines drove through the breastplate of his armour and into his flank. The pain forced him to release the grip of his weapon, but he soon recovered. He grabbed the marine's helmet and quickly snapped his neck.

Jones reached down to the Assegai and pulled it out while facing away from the others. The helmet at least hid his gritted teeth and pain from them. The Assegai had his blood on it, but he holstered it as his before turning to the others. Parker immediately noticed the hole in his armour.

"How bad is it?" she asked.

"I'm fine. Come on, we're running out of time!"

He didn't feel fine at all. Even the burning hot Assegai had not completely sealed the wound, and he could feel the clamminess of his own blood expanding within his uniform. He knew he couldn't hide the wound from the others for long, but it didn't matter to him in that moment. He looked back at his Mappad; they were just a short distance away.

A broad corridor-width blast door lay ahead of them. As they approached, it opened to bring a shocking sight that brought them to an instant halt. More than twenty enemy marines had deployed hard defences across the corridor width and were set up with heavy weapons. Jones no longer had his shield, like many others in his unit. Their hasty rush for the target had cost them assets, which now they regretted. They might as well have been standing in front of a firing squad.

"Lay down your weapons!" one of the enemy officers cried.

It was a line Jones was getting all too bored of hearing. Everyone wanted Taylor alive. *You would have thought they would have learned by now?*

"What do you want to do?" Parker asked quietly.

Jones looked back and could see there was no cover at all.

"We can't give up, or it was all for nothing," said Herrera.

"And if we die here and now, is it any better?" asked

Parker.

"Put your fucking weapons down!"

"We surrender we are dead anyway. We rush them, and some of us might live. You know what to do," said Jones.

They knew he'd say that, but none wanted to hear it.

"Ready on my go."

He looked back to the gun line and knew it would probably be the last thing he ever saw. "Why on earth do I volunteer for this shit?" he grumbled, which brought a few smiles from the others.

"Now!"

Jones leapt forward, but as he readied his rifle to fire, the line up ahead lit up with gun flashes. Jones expected to die any second as he rushed forward, but then through the muzzle flashes he could see it was not them firing, but their position being hit by a volley of fire from behind. A few of the marines tried to turn back but were cut down with no protection at all from their defences.

The platoon reached the line to find it was utterly devastated, and there stood Silva and his platoon. Silva's faceplate was up, and he looked more than a little pleased with himself.

"Damn that's some fine timing, Sergeant Major," said Jones sternly.

"Always."

CHAPTER TEN

Taylor's breathing was slow and he appeared calm while watching them pass the vast hull of the Nassau. He had to keep telling himself to breathe. They were passing so close to the battleship they could see the gunports, which was more than a little disconcerting. He was standing over the pilot and realised he didn't even know his name, despite knowing his face well. He couldn't see his nametag from where he stood either.

"How long till those systems recover?" Taylor asked.

"Not long now."

That's a big help, he thought. Though he knew the pilot wouldn't have any better idea than he did. They reached the far side of the hull and passed on out into the blackness once more. As they did so, the defence grid was revealed to them. It was a vast complex and many kilometres wide. It looked like a chain of ships orbiting the planet, which it effectively was.

"Nobody thought EMP shielding on the grid would be a good idea?" asked the pilot.

"It has backup systems as protection, but nothing like the Nassau. It's expensive kit that nobody wanted to pay for."

"Serious?"

It was the rumour he had heard, and it made as much sense as anything else, so he simply agreed, although fully aware that was exactly the way ridiculous scuttlebutt spread, but it at least brought a small smile to his face to know for once he was the one perpetuating such rumours.

"The other two still with us?" asked Taylor.

"Affirmative."

"All right, bring us in slow, as little power as you can manage."

Taylor saw just a small amount of light from the side of the cockpit from one of the other ship's engines firing up.

"That's not good," said the pilot.

Taylor turned to look ahead and saw a frigate float into their path.

"We're on a collision course unless we do something. Too much power, and we'll easily be spotted with the amount of light we'll put out."

"Just do what you can."

The pilot made just a few adjustments as they soared towards the warship.

"I hope this is gonna be enough."

A bright light flashed beside them, as one of the pilots reacted more vigorously to take evasive manoeuvres.

"Idiot," said the pilot.

They both knew the other pilot had gone too far, but there was nothing they could do about it now. It was every crew for themselves. They watched the nose of their ship passed within a few metres of the top deck of the frigate. Taylor waited for the sound of impact any second, but they had made it past. Just as he thought they had got through without a hitch, he heard the last thing he wanted to.

"We got a problem."

Taylor looked down at the console but didn't know what he was looking at.

"The Nassau's systems have fully recovered. We…" A bright flash cut him off, and the ship with them that had taken evasive manoeuvres exploded. Taylor looked out. There was nothing left bar some debris floating about space. He dipped and shook his head.

Twenty-five souls lost, many of them members of Inter-Allied who have served with us for years.

The thought made him sick to the stomach, but the pilot interrupted his thought process.

"They're tracking us. Almost got a lock…"

"What? I thought you were flying under the radar?"

"I don't know what to tell you, Colonel. We've been

had."

"Full power now, evasive action!"

The pilot hesitated after what had happened to the other ship.

"Look, we either sit here and die, or we take our chances!"

The pilot quickly reacted this time and put full power to the engines. There was another frigate up ahead, and they were sticking to it like glue.

"They've got a lock on us. This is gonna be close!"

Taylor felt helpless, knowing they were all in the hands of the one pilot and luck now. A flash of light zoomed past them, and they knew it was a shot from the Nassau that would have ended them.

"Almost there," whispered the pilot.

Their ship rushed over the frigate, and the pilot quickly brought them to a standstill behind the cover of the powerless ship.

"What are you doing?" asked Taylor.

"We can't go back out there. We'll never make it."

"We can't wait here, or it was all for nothing."

"And is us all dying for nothing worth something?"

Taylor couldn't help but agree, but they desperately needed to do something. He looked down at his watch and at how little time they had left to complete their mission. There were no options left, and in that instance, he drew his pistol and put it to the pilot's head.

"What the hell are you doing?"

Taylor was utterly calm as he responded.

"Full power, get us to our target now!"

"You'll kill us all."

"Either go now and maybe survive, or I'll shoot you down and figure it out myself."

He was getting desperate, and it started to look that he may well actually shoot the man. That was enough to convince the pilot.

"You're insane," he said, putting the power down, and they soared forward. Gunfire rushed past them, and then a red warning light flashed in the cockpit.

"Incoming missiles, deploying countermeasures. Our luck won't hold forever, Colonel!"

As he said it, everything went quiet, and the shots stopped. They both looked at the viewing screen displaying the Nassau with utter shock.

"He's done it. Jones has done it," said Taylor.

He knew it was the only reason the firing would stop. As he said it, they saw a burning ship pass them at speed and barrelling out of control. Troops were bailing out from the rear door. He knew it was Captain Grey's ship. He was amazed they had made it at all.

"Good luck to you," he muttered.

"Poor bastards," added the pilot.

"Poor? They're alive, aren't they? They'll reach the station, no problem. It's us you should be worried about.

We're on our own now," said Taylor, as he holstered his pistol. "Take us in as planned, and then get yourself a rifle. You're coming with us."

All the army pilots had been training for infantry combat, but none of them ever expected to physically be involved in it. The pilot looked horrified.

"You just flew through hell, and you're okay with that, but getting your boots on the ground scares you?"

"You shoot, I fly. It's the way I like to keep it."

"Well, tough shit. Today you are whatever I need you to be."

Taylor was ever bit as terrified as the pilot, but he'd never show it.

"You really expecting me to take up a rifle?"

"Bet your ass, I need every fighter I can get."

He looked back, expecting to see Jafar close in behind in support, forgetting he was with Jones. For all the time he had grown to hate the aliens, it now felt strange to go into combat without one.

"Nassau is launching fighters and transports," said the pilot.

"It's fine. They can't stop us now."

They were coming in for their final descent to the defence grid. It was an intimidating sight to fly past lines of railguns and other weaponry. A single salvo from any one of the towers would end them before they could even see it coming. Knowing they were disabled didn't calm their nerves an awful lot. Just twenty seconds later, they made their landing on one of the maintenance doors as planned.

"Good work," said Taylor, holding out his hand in friendship to the pilot he had so recently held a gun too.

"Spears," replied the pilot. "Lieutenant Spears."

He wished they would all live long enough that it was worth knowing the man's name. The ship had come to a halt, but nobody made a move. He wasn't sure if they were waiting for his order or if they were afraid.

"We're almost there, almost through. The World is looking to us. Just the few of us, so let's not let them down. You've held true for Jones all these years, will you now follow me to victory?"

Many of them nodded, but there was no roar of excitement and approval, as he would have expected of his marines. Jones' men were disciplined like no others and their cool silence laconic.

"Open the door, prepare to breach," he ordered.

They leapt into action and clamped the charges onto the doors of the maintenance bay.

"Fire when ready."

The shaped charges made a short and controlled blast that had almost no echo at all. Taylor looked in through the breach, half expecting to be met by a gun line, but the entrance was clear. He stepped inside and found the emergency lighting was already on. It struck him as suspicious, for he did not expect any systems to be operational anytime soon.

"How the hell have they got power?"

He turned to see nobody gave a response. They had no better idea than he. He didn't know whether to be glad they had made it safely, or terrified they were stepping into something they couldn't handle. Either way there was no choice in the matter now. He carried on through the corridor until they came out near a bank of massive capacitors. He could only imagine they were a part of the power systems of the weaponry they passed on the way in.

The room was opening up, and the ceilings were now ten metres high. It was nothing like a ship he'd ever been on. It was more like a power station back on Earth. Two metre-wide cylinders reached up from the floor to the ceiling like rows of columns, but none of it meant anything to the Colonel, other than as a marker he recognised from the research he had done en route.

"Freeze! Colonel Jones of the Inter-Allied Regiment, you are under arrest! Lay down your weapons, and no harm will come to you!"

Taylor couldn't tell where the call had come from, but he jumped to the nearest column for cover as he tried to find the source. It was at least a little relief they didn't know his true identity.

"Someone ran us into a trap," said Herbert.

"Maybe, but they were always gonna be protecting this

place."

There was total silence for a moment, and they looked around for some sign of an enemy presence.

"Lay down your weapons, and this will end without bloodshed!"

Then Taylor noticed it was coming from a tannoy system in one corner.

"They've got us on camera. Damn! We're gonna have a shit load of trouble coming down on us real soon."

He expected a response from those with him, but then he forgot they were British, and they waited for his command. He looked around for the cameras which were giving away their position, but they were clearly too small and well hidden, but he also knew the defence platform was vast enough that they could only cover so many areas.

"Let's move now!"

Taylor jumped out into a quick pace hoping he was right. No gunshots ensued, and he knew he must be. They passed on into a room full of yet more hardware that meant nothing to him. Taylor knew exactly what he was looking for, and that was all that mattered.

They knew they were running on borrowed time, but none of them expected to be caught up with so soon when they heard a string of gunshots up ahead. They were forced to duck for any cover they could find. Shots zipped past Taylor's head, and he tried to get a fix on how many they were facing. He could already count a dozen rifles being fired ahead of them. He looked to Harris who was up against the pillar beside him.

"Any good ideas, Corporal?"

Harris shook his head. "No way around them, Sir. We'll have to go through them."

That's not what I wanted to hear, but what choice do we have?

Taylor drew out a flashbang from his armour and held it for just a second while he gave out his orders through their comms. "Flash, then forward." It was simple, but he knew they would understand exactly what he meant. He threw out the grenade, and the vast room was lit up with a blinding glow. He knew many of their attackers would have had time to get to cover, but it was better than nothing. He leapt out with his shield held before him and rushed forward.

As he closed the distance, he could see the cover they were using also limited the enemy's arc of fire, and he was heading for just two enemy combatants. It was enough to spur him on in the knowledge his shield would protect him. As he ran, he threw a frag grenade with all the strength his suit would afford him. It bounced along the floor in front of him. One of the soldiers leapt for cover, but the other had not noticed.

The Colonel was little more than five metres from the grenade when it ignited. The soldier disappeared in the blast. Taylor felt the impact halve his pace and almost cause him to be thrown from his feet. He reached the source of the blast where the body of the fallen soldier was sprawled out across the ground and riddled with shrapnel, but as he turned to find the other, his helmet connected with a gun barrel.

"Don't move!"

He tilted his head just a few millimetres, enough to see hit attacker. The rifle barrel was touching his face and would be enough to kill him, should the soldier fire. He looked down at the man's uniform to see he was a member of Col Moshin, the 9th Parachute Assault Battalion. He had heard of the Italian Special Forces but never met them. It got questions rolling around in his head about their mission, but he knew he must first deal with the matter at hand.

Taylor wanted to reveal who he was and try to plead with the man to see sense, but he knew he could not. His identity must remain a secret for as long as possible.

"What are you doing here?" asked Taylor. "Do you want to see whole cities wiped out by these weapons?"

"Put down your weapon!" the soldier replied.

"You have to know you're on the wrong side in this war?"

"Put down your weapon!" he yelled, just a few decibels higher.

A man who stuck to his principles, something which could be respected in all other walks of life, except when they were Taylor's enemy. Harris rushed into view with several other of his platoon. The Italian soldier pulled

Taylor in close, using him as a human shield.

"Let him go!" screamed Harris. His faceplate was raised from where he was clearly trying to get a little more air than his suit was providing. Taylor wished he could have such a luxury. Harris looked ready to fire at a moment's notice, and that was never going to endear the Italian to them.

"Put down your weapons or he dies."

There was no option left but for Taylor to get out of it himself. His rifle was slung on his back and out of reach, and he could not stretch across his Assegai or reach down for his sidearm without raising attention. His shield was still attached to his arm, and he knew it was his best bet. He looked down to see the Italian's foot beside him, and in one quick action smashed the shield down onto his foot.

The impact was hard enough it cracked the cap of the boot and crushed several bones in the man's foot. He screamed in pain as he fell back, and his rifle fired a single shot that went only a few centimetres high of the Colonel. Taylor swung the shield around. He smashed it with both hands into the man, knocked him off his feet, and launched him into the air until his head connected with a support beam. His body passed beneath, snapping his neck, and he dropped limply to the floor.

He turned back and could see Harris looking impressed, although he would never admit it. He was surprised the action had been over so quick.

"How many were there?"

"Four."

"Four? That was it?"

He knew in that moment that they were good. They had presented the image of a much larger threat than they really were, and against most other units it would have worked. But Taylor was either too experienced or too desperate to have been stopped by the danger.

"What the hell are they even doing up here? Special Forces on a guard duty?"

"I don't think they were sent here to guard anything. I think they were sent to hunt whoever came aboard, and I'd be willing to bet we'll see plenty more trouble coming our way before this is over."

* * *

"How much longer do we have to hold?"

"Until the job is done, Parker!" snapped Jones.

He rose up from their barricade and fired a few more shots. As he ducked back down, he was suddenly struck with how bizarre it felt to fight an enemy who were fearful of advancing and scared of death.

Fighting humans isn't all bad, he thought to himself, but he soon realised he didn't believe it. Parker slid back her visor to let some air in.

"Think Taylor made it?"

Jones wanted to believe he had, the same as the rest of them.

"If anyone can do it, he can."

At least it was what Parker wanted to hear.

The gunfire from their enemy suddenly stopped, and with it, so did their own as they no longer had any targets. Jones knew they hadn't beaten their attackers, so it only made him feel uncomfortable.

"What are they doing?" asked Herrera.

"Whatever it is, it can't be good," replied Parker.

As she said it, they heard the familiar heavy footsteps of Mech soldiers stomping towards them. Parker shook her head in disbelief. "Not this again."

Gunshots rang out before she'd even finished, and they were quick to respond. Jones took aim when he saw dozens of Mechs were pouring towards them. As they knocked a few down, they could see human soldiers behind, using the Mechs as a screen to cover ground. Explosions rang out, hitting all around them, and they were soon engulfed in smoke used to further screen the enemy advance.

Seconds later, a Mech rushed through the smoke over their barricade and came at Jones, firing and with no intent to stop. Jones leapt out of the line of fire and smashed the Mech's weapon aside with the barrel of his own, but it was not enough to stop the charge of the creature. It tumbled into him and knocked him to the ground, toppling onto him and almost crushing him to death.

Jones struck forward at the faceplate of the Mech's armour, but his hardest strike was not enough to break through. He tried to reach for his Assegai, but he was pinned under the alien and its weapon. It raised itself up for just a moment so that it could strike down with a thunderous blow towards his head. It would have been enough to crush his helmet and kill him instantly.

He took the split second opportunity he had to kick up with his legs and throw the Mech sideways. The creature's fist smashed into the floor barely a few centimetres from his head and dented the floor beside him. He drew his Assegai with his left hand and thrust it into the creature's stomach. It recoiled in pain, but then spun around and struck out with its last breath. The strike hit Jones' helmet and knocked him out cold.

* * *

Taylor was still on the move and every second praying they could make it in time. It was still a long way to the centre of the vast facility when they came up against warning signs of high explosives. He stopped; they were inside a vast missile silo.

"These go off with gunfire?" he asked.

Sergeant Herbert shrugged his shoulders, as none of them knew for sure.

"All right, we can't take the chance. Rifles down.

Nobody fires a shot until we're free and clear."

He let his rifle hang down at his side and drew out his Assegai.

"Why don't we just blow this place from here?" asked Harris.

Taylor thought about it for a moment. He wanted nothing more than to put an end to it there and then and be on his way, but he thought back to what they had seen on their route in. Taking out a single silo could not destroy the vast complex. It would be isolated from the grid and do little to help.

"No, we stick to the plan."

He felt more than a little vulnerable and naked without his rifle in hand. They were going deeper and deeper into enemy territory with just a handful of fighters. He was anxious now, scared even. He tried hard to keep his breathing in check and put one foot in front of the other. It was when he thought of Parker and Jones and all his others comrades aboard the Nassau that his willpower really kicked in.

The platoon took a bend and found a line of guns trained on them. They froze for a moment, but no shots were fired. Taylor pointed to the warning signs that were all around.

"A single shot could blow us all to hell!"

Thirty Italian soldiers stood in front of them ready to open fire, but they turned their attention to what Taylor was pointing to.

"He's bluffing!" one of them said.

"Look around you!" he shouted back.

He could see the panic start to kick in, but they soon lowered their rifles and drew out Assegais.

"Step aside or you'll all die here," said Taylor.

He had no desire to fight them, but neither could he afford to have them stand in his way. No response came, so he strode forward with his shield at the ready. He knew they would make light work of the soldiers who were without shields or the experience of his own troops. Nevertheless, they stood their ground, and when their officer commanded, charged forward.

Taylor ducked under and launched the first soldier over his shield and back into his own ranks. He parried off an Assegai coming at him with his own and kicked the soldier back before driving his own into the flank of another. He did not stop to engage a single one of the troops but worked his way through, allowing the rest of his comrades to get stuck in.

By the time he reached the back rank, two of the troops threw down their weapons and ran.

"Let them go," said Taylor.

He knew they were terrified enough not to cause any further trouble. He looked back to see the carnage they had created. The floor was thick with human blood and bodies. He did not feel the triumph and pleasure he had when cutting his way through Mechs. It made him feel sick to know he had to do the same to his own people.

"Any casualties?" he asked.

"One dead," replied Herbert sternly.

"One more than we can afford right now," he replied.

Taylor didn't even have time to ask the name of the fallen. He turned and carried on. He knew they couldn't be too far now, but as they passed into a broad corridor, they heard a large mechanical lurch and looked ahead at the blast doors that were shutting.

"Come on! Run!" he screamed. They rushed at a full sprint for the doorways, but they were closing rapidly. He was at the head of the column and jumped through with ease. Herbert got through after him and two privates, one of which bounced off the doorway and narrowly missed being trapped in the door as he was catapulted into Taylor.

All went silent as the doors sealed shut.

"Sorry, Sir," insisted the Private.

Taylor helped the man to his feet and could see his name, Private Little, and the other beside him Private Ball. "Shit," he said to himself. "We're losing numbers at a hell of a rate."

"We need to get these doors open sharpish," said Ball.

"If only, but you saw their depth. More than we can expect to handle anytime soon. We've no choice but to go on," replied Taylor.

"Go on with four men?"

"If only one of us makes it there and gets the job done, then so be it, Ball."

Taylor turned and led the way. He knew their chances of success with so few were slim now, but he had no choice than to continue. He wanted nothing more than to rip his helmet off and get past the stifling effect of it, but he could not, and he had to bear it for now. The stale smell and taste of his own sweat was killing him now.

Just a little longer, he told himself.

"You really think we can do this, Sir?"

"Wouldn't be here if I didn't think we could, Private Little."

"Sometimes I just think you hope for the best and fight like hell to make it happen, Sir," added Herbert.

Taylor was surprised to hear the Sergeant speak, let alone what he said. He couldn't help but smile.

"Yeah, well, it's worked so far."

He prayed the others would find a way to reach them, as well as Grey, but he already suspected they were on their own. It was in that moment he thought back to the gladiatorial fights where he had been paraded about. He felt so alone before such massive crowds, and yet he didn't now with just a handful of comrades and surrounded by those who wanted to kill him.

This is my natural habitat, he told himself. *I am the hunter here.* He was trying to psych himself up to overcome the fear, and it was working.

A pulsating sound rang through the corridor around them. Full lighting came on, and a security turret on the ceiling ahead rotated around and took aim.

"Cover!" he shouted.

They scattered each side of the corridor as shots hit the ground.

"They've got full power back!"

He tried to get up to fire, but shots quickly smashed all around him with one glancing off the top of his helmet. He pushed his shield out from cover enough so he could use the transparent view port on it, and then put his rifle out on top and used his targeter. Three shots hit the shield, but he was not deterred. He took careful aim and then fired a three-shot burst into the security turret, and it blew apart.

"If they have power back, we're in deep trouble," stated Herbert.

"What do you mean?" Little asked.

"With the defence grid operational and under the control of the UEN, our fleet will have to break off its attack. Without the fleet, our forces aboard the Nassau are done for, and the UEN can use this thing to fire on whatever targets it wants."

"Should take some time for them to power up the big guns," replied Herbert.

"Yeah, I figure we got about ten minutes until they're ready to vaporise any city they want."

"What do we do, Sir?" asked Ball.

"The only thing we can do, what we came here to do. We have to disable this system."

"But with four of us, how?"

"We aren't far now. We may not have much time to stop this, but neither do they have a lot of time to bring in reinforcements. Speed is the only thing we have on our side. Let's take this fucker down now!"

They all agreed, and Taylor led them on. Up ahead was a broad domed intersection, exactly as he was expecting.

"Only half a klick from here now. We're almost there!"

They reached the entrance to the intersection and turned to the left as they needed to but were halted by a shocking sight. The Mechs stood guarding the entrance. They each wore a modified form of Reitech weapons bolted to their arms and shields twice the size of that Taylor carried.

"Oh, shit…"

CHAPTER ELEVEN

Jones regained consciousness to see lights flashing around him, but his hearing was a little more delayed while he came to his senses. He did not recognise where they were, and it certainly was not where he had been fighting the last he remembered. Parker appeared before him and slapped him in the face, which did at least something to wake him.

"Good, you're back. We need you."

He looked around at several dead and wounded. As his hearing returned, he could hear a furious gun battle going on.

"Where are we? Why aren't we defending the target?"

"We couldn't hold there. They sent Mechs in against us, and we couldn't hold."

"But Taylor, if we didn't keep their weapons from firing, he will never make it."

"If he hasn't made it by now, he never was gonna."

He tried to take it all in for a moment, but he was still a little stunned.

"We have to take back our positions and stop their weapon systems, or King and the others won't be able to reach us."

"How? We're being hammered," she replied.

Jones could hear the desperation in her voice.

"Taylor is aboard the grid, and if he can't stop it, then it's all for nothing now anyway. We just have to survive!" she added.

"We have to get a message to Taylor," said Jones.

"How? With the jamming in place here, we can't even dream of it."

"But if we can reach the Nassau's own comms systems, we will be able to communicate with him directly, won't we?"

"I guess so."

"He has to know what has happened here and that nobody is coming to his aid!"

"Why?"

"He needs to know he's our only hope now."

She beckoned for Herrera to come over to her.

"We need a line of communications off this boat, and we need it now!"

He looked confused.

"We'll need access to their systems for that."

"Where can we get it?"

"I think I know where, but getting there is a different matter."

"I'd rather die going forward than being cornered here," stated Jones. "Set charges on that far wall. Leave the wounded with plenty of ammunition to keep up the fight while we go onwards."

"Leave the wounded? Those Mechs won't show mercy," replied Herrera.

Jones grabbed him by the shoulder. "Does it look like they're showing any mercy at the moment? Get to it!"

He did as ordered without any further questioning.

"You really believe he's still alive, don't you?"

"Of course he's still alive, Eli. If the World was afire, and humanity facing extinction, Taylor would be the last bitter survivor unwilling to give in to death."

Jones picked up his rifle, slammed in a new magazine, and got to his feet. His knees wobbled a little as he did so, and Parker grabbed onto him.

"You okay?"

He shook it off and nodded before kneeling down and pulling a shield from one of their dead. It was a grim thing to have to do, to salvage equipment from fallen comrades, but he had no choice.

"We should never have come here," said Parker. "We've done some crazy things, but to think we could take on all this and win? Either we bit off more than we could chew, or someone wants to see an end to Taylor and the Inter-

Allied."

"Perhaps getting the reputation as miracle workers isn't always a good thing," Jones laughed.

A massive explosion tore through the room as Herrera ignited the charges without them hearing any warning. Dust and debris filled the room as Jones rushed to the hole in the wall. He stopped for just a split second to peer into where they were heading before taking the leap. They were in a storage facility stacked to the roof with crates.

"Lead the way!" Jones hollered to Herrera.

The two were side by side as they headed for the nearest entrance they could see. Jones looked back, and he had about twenty others with him at the most. As they reached the exit, a Mech stepped into view just a metre from them. Jones didn't even break stride. He leapt up and threw his entire weight at the creature's torso, and it tumbled out of the room. As they rolled over one another, Jones gained his footing and put the barrel of his rifle into its face. He fired a five-shot burst, killing it instantly.

Blue blood spurted out from the gaping holes, and it felt good to see after having so much human blood spilt on both sides. He looked either side, but there were no other enemies in sight.

"Must have been a sentry. Let's move!"

He followed Herrera on down into a corridor and a few other rooms without seeing any further contact.

"This is it!" Herrera called out.

It was a sealed security door to a communications room. "Anyone got any explosives left?"

They all shook their heads, but Jafar came storming towards the door. He fired a burst of gunfire into one spot where the edge met the frame, and then pushed his fingers into the slot and yanked it from its hinges. The huge door sprung across the corridor, narrowly missing Jones and hit the wall with a resonating clatter before smashing to the ground.

Jones stepped inside to see two personnel sitting at their workstations. They were too scared to even reach for their weapons and merely sat with their mouths open as Jafar stepped into the room.

"Do as we ask, and no harm will come to you!" Jones said.

They nodded in agreement, but they still quivered in fear. Jones ripped his helmet off. He knew his identity no longer mattered, and he needed to feel something resembling fresh air. He took in a deep breath, wiped the sweat from his brow, and clipped the helmet onto his belt.

"You aren't.... Colonel Taylor," one of them insisted.

"Shut up and do as I ask of you," he replied. "I want a direct communicate to a personal comms unit off ship."

They did not answer.

"I know you can do it, so don't make me ask again."

Jafar stepped a little closer and stood intimidatingly over them.

"Okay, okay," said one. She was a short petite woman and looked like a child compared to Jafar who loomed over her. Jones tapped a few keys on his Mappad and then walked over and held it in front of her.

"This is who I want to speak to."

"No way this is gonna be a safe line," said Parker.

"Nope, but it doesn't matter anymore."

The comms operator put in the details, and a moment later the call was accepted. A repeated heavy banging noise came over the speakers like metal beating on metal, until finally they heard Taylor's voice.

"Who the hell is this?" he asked.

"This is Jones."

"Yeah, right, you won't fool me again, you assholes."

Parker interrupted.

"Mitch, it's Eli. This is legit."

"Eli? How the hell did you get this message through?"

"Don't have time to explain right now," added Jones. "The Nassau is now fully operational, and there is nothing we can do about it. You're on your own."

The video screen flickered before them as Taylor activated his camera feed on his Mappad.

"What sort of shape are you in?"

"Still standing, Mitch," though Taylor knew it wasn't good.

"Can you still disable the defence grid?" Jones asked.

Taylor had the look of defeat on his face, and they

could all tell from the background on the video he was hold up somewhere and with few people left.

"I can try."

Parker began to speak, but gunfire lit up the room, and Taylor lost the feed.

"Eli? Jones!" There was nothing. He looked around to the other three who were with him. They looked as lost as he did. They were locked in a large empty storage facility. Mechs were banging on the door, trying to get through and kill them.

"If we stay here, we die. If we open that door, we may well die," he stated.

"I'm not dying up here," said Herbert.

"If we don't get past these bastards, it was all for nothing. We might as well have put our feet up in France and watched the whole World go to hell. I don't know about you, but the idea we did all this for nothing sure pisses me off."

They all nodded in agreement.

"We're gonna open this door, and we're gonna take these bastards down anyway we can, you got it?"

"Hell, yes," Little replied.

"Sergeant, be ready on that door."

They each took up positions and held up their shields ready for the onslaught.

"On my go… now!"

The thick steel doors slid apart, revealing nine creatures

that did not hesitate to charge at them. Shots were fired from arm mounted weapon systems. Taylor leapt into the air over the first and spun in the air firing a burst in the head of his attacker before descending on the next one. As he landed on the Mech's shoulders, it threw its shield up at him.

Taylor was thrown off the creature, and his rifle snapped in half by the impact. He rolled across the floor and back up onto one knee, just in time to see two of the Mechs rushing towards him. From his flank, Herbert crashed into one of the Mechs and sent it tumbling into the other. Taylor seized the moment and rushed forward, frantically stabbing the nearest one several times before it could get to its feet. Herbert did the same.

They looked up to see Private Ball being pushed back and fending off strong thrusts from two of the Mechs. They were using a version of the Assegai twice the length of their own. Little was nowhere to be seen, but another three Mechs were rushing at him. Taylor passed off a thrust from one of them with his shield, but as he attempted to counter, the creature tried to crush him with its vast shield.

Taylor was knocked down onto one knee, barely managing with both hands to hold up his shield from the crushing blow. All he could see now were the Mechs' feet. He thrust his Assegai into the nearest and then drove up and stabbed again into the upper thigh area, pushing forwards with his shield until the creature was knocked onto its back and unable to support its own weight.

Mitch landed on the beast, but it had its shield dividing them just as he had done. Before he could strike again, the Mech pushed its shield up and launched him up like he'd come off a springboard. As he flew up, the Mech staggered to get to his feet, and he could see he was going come back down on the creature; it was waiting to stab him with its weapon. He gave his boosters a little kick to alter course, turned to land behind the Mech, and with all the strength he could muster, thrust his Assegai into its back.

He could tell it was dead because he felt the weight begin to fall back against him. In disgust, he pushed forward which threw the body down onto the floor face down. Mitch turned back and saw Herbert was repeatedly stabbing his opponent where it still stood. Taylor spun around and found Ball backed against a wall by the last remaining Mech. He could see one he had already killed on the floor a few metres from him.

Taylor threw his Assegai across the room, hitting Ball's attacker between the shoulder blades. The creature recoiled for a moment and then staggered until it toppled to the floor. But as it unblocked his view of Ball, he could see the Private was pinned against the wall by the creature's Assegai. The weapon was driven through his thick armour at the abdomen.

"No," whispered Taylor.

He and Herbert rushed to the Private and removed his helmet. Blood was gushing from his mouth. The weapon that had gone through him was thicker than a scaffold pole, and they both knew there was no hope.

"Sorry, Sir," he muttered, as even more blood spat out from his mouth.

Taylor could see the Private had killed one of his attackers and wounded the other before being struck.

"No, I am sorry. Don't you apologise for anything. You fought hard and you fought well."

It left a bitter taste in Taylor's mouth that he had only gotten to know the dying man that day, despite having served together for so long.

"You won't die for nothing, Ball. We came here to get the job done, and you better believe we're gonna do it."

Ball nodded, but he could no longer speak. He took his last breath and died still pinned to the wall.

"Damn fine soldier, Sir," said Herbert.

"They all were, everyone we have ever lost."

"Help, help me," came a muted call.

They had forgotten about Little, and they could hear him pleading for assistance. They walked back through the dead towards the sound until they found another Mech. The voice was coming from underneath, and they could see Little's left arm and shield stuck out from beneath the body.

"Help me," said Taylor.

The two of them got down low and pushed until the creature toppled over to one side and revealed the Private trapped below. His Assegai was embedded in the lifeless creature.

"I'm alive!" he cried ecstatically.

Herbert hauled him to his feet, but the smile was quickly removed when he saw the body of Ball.

"Fuckers, mother fuckers, they killed him!"

Taylor grabbed the Private and shook him until he was silenced.

"We've all lost a lot of friends against these bastards, but this isn't the time to cry over them. Pick up your weapon, and let's do what we came to do."

It was a sobering message that the Private reluctantly accepted. He drew out the Assegai and stared at the blue blood dripping down over his gloves.

"I'm gonna kill them all. I'm gonna kill every fucking alien!"

"Then follow me."

"They must know by now you have made it here and are not aboard the Nassau," said Herbert.

"Surely. All that remains is the question, can they stop us?"

"Stop us? No one can stop us!" screamed Small.

He was psyched up and ready to kill, just as he needed to be. The main control deck for the defence grid was up ahead, and they stopped on seeing what was guarding it; Elite Krys Mechs, just like Jafar and Tsengal. Their presence sent a chill down Taylor's spine, for he knew where they go, so do Alien Lords.

Where the hell is Jafar when you need him? Taylor thought.

"Can we take 'em?" asked Herbert.

"We don't have a choice."

As he said it, a door opened at their flanks, and twenty metres inside were twenty Mechs.

"Oh, shit," Taylor sighed.

He knew they were done for now, but in that moment Little did something both suicidal and incredible. He raised his shield up and sprinted for the Mechs.

"No!" Taylor hollered.

It was too late.

"Come on, you square headed bastards!" the Private screamed.

As he passed through the door, he punched the release switch. The doors began to shut, and they saw a few flashes as Private Little blew out the control switch and cut the creatures off. Taylor thought he had gone made with bloodlust for the loss of his friend, but he'd also given them the only chance they would get.

Taylor turned to Herbert in surprise, but the Sergeant showed nothing but pride for what his man had done.

Two against two, Taylor thought to himself, *not bad odds.*

The two Krys soldiers wore agile and close fitting

armour, just as Jafar and Tsengal had. It was adorned with elaborate silver symbols and detailing. It reminded him of the last time he had seen Demiran; the day he had killed the alien Lord. But these symbols were different. He assumed they must serve a different Lord, and that was a terrifying prospect.

'Think you can handle this?" he asked Herbert.

The Sergeant didn't reply, but he looked confident enough it was an answer in itself. The two creatures were armed differently with what appeared to be their own unique weapons. He studied them, and they stepped out into the open room to face off against the two humans.

One carried a pole weapon two metres long, with what looked like an iron ball one end and a double headed axe the other. The other dropped a hollowed out sphere to the floor. It had spikes protruding from every angle and a chain running up to the creature's grip. In its other hand it carried a metre-long curved blade that was glowing from some energy source connected to the alien's suit.

"We get past these bastards, and we've got a free run at it. They are all that stands in our way; all that stands in the way of the success of this mission. One of us has to make it through."

The two creatures simply stood their ground, blocking the path they had to take, and waiting for Taylor and Herbert to come to them. He couldn't decide which he'd rather fight less because both looked ready to take his head clean off. He turned to Herbert and nodded. It was all that the Sergeant needed to see as confirmation to attack. He jumped towards the pole weapon-wielding alien, firing on full auto as he did.

The alien leapt aside to dodge the rounds and swung the massive weapon around towards Herbert's legs. The Sergeant jumped at the last moment, but only one leg fully cleared the weapon. The shaft clipped his other leg and sent him into a tumble. His rifle was smashed as he crashed over it, but he landed back on one knee with his hand already on his Assegai.

It was Taylor's turn now. He went forward but didn't know quite what to expect from the beast. Then with lightning speed the Mech snapped the chain, and the ball of the weapon came flying directly for his head. He moved his shield over barely in time, and the ball struck the corner taking it clean off. The impact was just enough to divert the weapon over Taylor's head. But as he continued on, the creature yanked the weapon back, and the ball smashed him in the back, almost taking him off balance.

In that moment, the alien swung the huge curved blade to his right side beyond the reach of his shield. He turned and quickly spun around in time to catch it with his shield and spin past the creature. Sparks flew from the shield, but the sword had cut halfway through his armour.

Shit!

He now stood three metres from the creature and knew

he had to close the distance. He circled it, and trying to find some way past the chain weapon that wouldn't see him cleaved in two by the sword. He heard beside him the clash of weapons as Herbert went forward. He had to rely on the Sergeant to take on the other; he was having a hard enough time against the one he was fighting.

Before he could think any longer, the ball came at him once again. He leapt aside and narrowly avoided it, but on the return it lashed around his shield, and the creature launched him through the air. He crashed into a wall and felt the wind knocked out of him.

That's it! I've had enough.

He got back up, holding the shield forward, and slipped his Assegai into his shield grip without the creature being able to see.

He circled the creature and waited for it to yank the chain back to throw at him once again. As it did, he moved his shield aside and drew his pistol like a gunslinger, firing three shots from the hip. Two of them struck the chain when it was at the moment of changing direction. It split apart and the bladed sphere was launched back across the room and embedded in the wall. Taylor smiled at his ingenuity and fine shooting, but the creature cried like a banshee, rushed at him and swung a quick and strong vertical strike. He dodged the blade that took a heavy slice into the floor, but a second later it was coming at him again.

He took the impact with his shield, and the blade carved in thirty centimetres, stopping just millimetres from his arm. This was his chance. With the blade embedded, he twisted the shield and levered it from the creature's grip. Simultaneously, he struck at the cable to the power source of the weapon with his Assegai and severed it from the creature's suit.

It worked, but the alien backhanded him a moment later. He was thrown to the ground, and the shield was tossed aside. The alien was unarmed now but came at him viciously. First it stamped down at him, but he rolled out of the way and back onto one knee, but a second kicked launched him through the air and against a wall. He was at least on his feet now.

"Come on, you ugly son of a bitch!" he shouted.

The alien did just that and rushed towards him, swinging a furious horizontal strike at him. The alien's anger was its undoing. He cool-headedly waited for the perfect moment, jumped over the attack, and took hold of the alien's neck. He rolled over and snapped the creature over onto its back. Instantly, and before it could recover, he drove his Assegai down into its chest. It let out a shriek in agony and punched him hard in the face. Taylor recoiled back and watched in amazement. The creature leapt back to its feet, pulled the weapon out, and tossed it aside.

"Die already," he muttered.

He had nothing left now. The beast came for him with

a hammer blow from above. He raised his arm to parry, but the weight of the blow shook his legs, fortunately not enough to make him fall. He punched with all his strength to the gushing open wound, and the beast fell back, cupping it in agony.

Taylor looked around for a weapon and noticed the bladed ball in the wall with much of the chain still attached. He grabbed the chain and ripped it out. It was the closest he'd had to holding a football since college and gave him a great idea. He launched it up and over the beast as it came at him, and then yanked the chain back. The weapon smashed into the back of the alien's head and dug in deep. It was dead at last and tumbled down to the floor.

With a sigh of relief, he looked over to Herbert. He was on one knee with his attacker standing over him. Both had a grip on the huge pole weapon the creature used.

"Right, you bastard," Taylor said.

He picked up his blood soaked Assegai, rushed at the creature, and drove it deep up into its rib cage. It swung around to get a hold of him, but he ducked under and stabbed again and again until it slumped dead. He offered out his hand to the Sergeant who was battered and bloody but still breathing.

"Time to end this," he stated.

The Sergeant gladly took his offer and was hauled to his feet. Taylor hit the button entry to the room they had fought so hard to reach, half expecting to find an army awaiting them, but there was no one.

"We're in luck," he said.

It was hard for either of them to believe, but they didn't want to question it. There were screens all around the room, showing both the interior and exterior of the ship. The very middle screen had all the ground targets programmed in, including over a dozen capitol cities."

"My God," Herbert said, "they were really going to do it."

"Colonel Taylor," said a deep and booming voice behind them. They both spun around with their weapons raised as their pulses pounded. An alien Lord stood before them who looked not unlike Demiran. His armour glistened as if lights shining on diamonds. Spikes protruded from every joint, but he not carry a weapon.

Before another word could be said, Taylor threw his Assegai for the alien's head. To his surprise it made no attempt to move. The blade passed through with no resistance or effect, striking a monitor behind the creature.

"It's a hologram," said Herbert.

Thank God, Taylor thought.

Neither of them had the strength to fight such an opponent.

"What do you want?"

"The question is what do you want?" he responded.

Great, an alien who speaks in fucking riddles. Now I get to be bored to death, too.

Taylor glanced at Herbert, knowing they must stay focused.

"You know what to do. Deactivate all weapon systems."

The Sergeant quickly complied and went for the main console.

"You have a choice, Colonel. Save millions of people, or save your friends."

Taylor didn't want to hear anymore of it, but the subject matter was one he could not ignore.

"All right, you ugly bastard. Quit beating about the bush, and say your piece."

In all honesty, he was terrified of the alien Lord's presence, as two had come close to killing him before, but he would not admit it or show fear in the face of another.

"I am Erdogan, and I have come to do what my counterparts could not."

Taylor knew the name, and he knew what that meant. The most powerful of the Krys Lords was here.

This can't be good. But he had no choice to play along.

"Go on…"

"In ten of your Earth minutes, the weapon systems of this device will destroy key cities of you and your allies. I have seen fit to isolate the key weapon systems from this grid so that they cannot be shut down remotely."

Taylor looked back to Herbert. The Sergeant looked horrified, and that was all the confirmation Taylor needed.

"What the hell do you want?"

Erdogan ignored the question and continued.

"I have been studying you, Colonel, for a long time now, and I know how to hurt you. In ten minutes, you may get to the other weapon systems and deactivate them. Or in those precious few minutes, you may get aboard the Nassau and save your friends. Jones, Parker, I know them all."

Taylor was frozen and began to shake and sweat with nervousness and anger. He rolled it over in his head and tried to find a way out.

"Your choice, Colonel, your friends or your planet. You have ten minutes."

As he said it, the hologram ended, and a timer started on the main screen in the room. He rushed over to the Sergeant who was frantically flicking through keys on a touch pad.

"What's our situation?"

"Silos 12 through 26 have been isolated from the system through two control points. If we go now, we may just reach them in time, but there is nothing we can do from here. Some of the nukes can be stopped by counter measures on the ground, but many are beam weapons that cannot be stopped."

He looked up to one of the monitors which displayed the Nassau and thought of his friends aboard.

"We have to go now, Colonel. That is what they would want. If we don't go now, millions will die!"

Taylor calmed his breathing and thought about it for a moment and then responded. "No, I won't do it. I won't let this bastard make me choose."

"What would you have us do?"

He froze for ten seconds, and Herbert grew more impatient.

"Do you still have control of the other silos?"

He looked down at the screens.

"Yeah, about half of them, why?"

He took a deep breath and answered. "Target silos 12 through 26, and destroy them immediately."

Herbert looked at him in disbelief.

"You want to destroy the defence grid? Those were not our orders."

"Not then, but things have changed somewhat, wouldn't you say?"

Herbert was silent.

"What will happen if we fire silo on silo?"

"I believe it will trigger automatic response systems. The silos would destroy one another."

"Then fire all but two."

Herbert looked confused.

"Just do it!"

The Sergeant punched in the targets and then held his hand over the authorisation switch to open fire. Taylor couldn't wait any longer and turned it himself. The two of them stepped back and watched as gun ports opened along the massive defence grid. Missiles flew across space and were soon met with beams smashing into parts of the station.

It was utter chaos and destruction; huge segments were blown apart and pulled into the Earth's atmosphere.

"We're in deep shit for this," stated Herbert.

"Only if we live through it," he replied.

Taylor looked at his watch. Three minutes had passed and their work on the defence grid was all but done.

"What now?" Herbert asked.

"With whatever we got left, target the power generators of the Nassau and take them out, along with any other nearby vessels."

Herbert opened his mouth to question it, but Taylor only stared back. He obliged and punched in the codes, and a salvo of fire erupted from what was left of the defence grid.

"You know how many trillions of dollars of stuff you just destroyed?" asked Herbert.

"Me? You pushed all the buttons."

Herbert looked a little pale.

"Our work here is done. Let's go and save the Regiment."

Herbert looked around as if to ask 'with what army?', but Taylor headed for the door anyway. He stopped on hearing gunfire, and out from another corridor in the intersection came Captain Grey. He was covered in blue blood and carrying a shield that had been carved in two, yet he still held it.

"Nice of you to finally join the party."

Lieutenant Spears strode out with him. They were little more than thirty in total.

"This is everyone?" asked Taylor.

Grey nodded grimly, and he could see they had suffered greatly fighting their way there. He understood now why they had met comparatively little resistance; Grey had taken the hits for them.

"Did you deactivate the weapons? Did you get it done?" asked Grey.

"In a fashion," muttered Herbert.

"It's a long story. Right now we need off this heap. We need to get aboard the Nassau. Know a way of making that happen?"

"There's a shuttle a little way back, nothing great but it should fly," stated Spears.

"Then lead the way. We're riding to the rescue of Jones, so buckle up because it's gonna be a rough ride!"

They rushed at speed behind Spears who was covering ground quickly and moving with real purpose. They reached the shuttle and found it was of civilian nature; shiny and new, but without any weapons or armour to speak of.

"How the hell are we going make it through an enemy fleet in this?" asked Grey.

"You'll see," replied Taylor with a smirk.

They were airborne in less than two minutes, but as they got out into space, the faces of the troops were of shock. They looked out at the debris of countless ships, and parts of the station they had been aboard burning.

"What the hell did you do?" Grey asked.

"What I had to, trust me."

Herbert was still shaking his head in astonishment.

"He put the lives of our Regiment before all others."

"What do you mean?"

"We probably could have shut down those weapons in the time we had, but we never could have saved Jones and the others. Taylor took out the weapons and gave us a clear path to the Nassau."

Grey shook his head in disbelief.

"What is it, Captain?" asked Taylor.

"This is gonna come back to bite us in the arse."

"Yeah, well, pretty much everything seems to. Let's just get our people out of there, and I'll call it a victory."

CHAPTER TWELVE

They were coming in for their final run to the Nassau, and Herbert still stared at Taylor. He knew what the glare was for. Erdogan. Taylor hadn't told the others, and they both knew it was a big deal. Taylor told himself it was a problem for another day and did his best to believe it.

"We're gonna have to head for one of the landing bays, no other way in!"

Taylor shrugged. "Whatever you gotta do, do it, Spears. It's as good a place to put down as any!"

"Going in hot without any fire support or armour, Colonel?"

"Got a better idea, Captain Grey?"

They both knew he was making it up as he went along, but neither could see any other options. They were down to improvising and overcoming all that was presented to them.

"This isn't going to be pretty," Spears whispered quietly.

They took a sharp turn into one of the open landing bays. There was only emergency lighting on and it cast long shadows. They could see glimmers of movement below, but nobody fired. It was clear no one had yet identified them as friend or foe, but Mitch couldn't bear being stuck in the metal coffin any longer.

"Put us down!"

Spears obliged, and they descended quickly to a bumpy ride and slid to a halt.

"Nice…" stated Grey.

"Hey, you want to fly next time, be my guest," cracked Spears.

Herbert was first at the door and punched the release switch. His face was still covered in his own blood, but he didn't seem to notice or care. He was eager and raring to go. He leapt out first and Taylor was close behind.

"What are we looking for?" asked Grey.

"Wherever all hell is breaking lose. That's where we'll find Jones."

That wasn't much to go on, but he got the idea. Taylor was still surprised nobody had started shooting at them. There was still a little movement further on down the bay, but the lighting was too low for them to be made out.

"We're in luck."

Grey shook his head. "You call us lucky, Colonel? I call us mugs."

Taylor got going, hoping in desperation that some of his marines were still alive. Although he was with comrades there and then, the closest of all his friends were somewhere deep inside the vessel and in God knows what state.

"You think they're still alive?"

"Of course, Jones, Jafar, Parker, Silva? They wouldn't go down lightly."

They all wanted to believe it was true, but none of them were immortal, no matter how much the World called them such. The room narrowed to a corridor barely a few people wide, and as they approached, they heard footsteps from a merging corridor. Taylor stopped and rested easy while the others held their rifles ready to fire. A few German marines appeared at the corridor merging with theirs and heading the same direction.

"You! Stop there!"

They did as Taylor had ordered, to everyone's surprise.

"Where are you heading, marine?"

The man looked uneasy, but looked at Taylor's rank and clearly felt compelled to answer.

"We're still fighting on F23L, Sir. They're dug in, and we haven't been able to shift them. We have been drafted in from the Bremen to assist."

As he was about to finish, Taylor drew his pistol, put it to the man's head, and grabbed him into an arm lock. The rest of his marines seemed too shocked to respond when

Grey and several others jumped into view with rifles held ready to fire.

"I am Colonel Mitch Taylor of the Inter-Allied Regiment. This fight is over. It is over because I said it is. And any man or woman who decides to stand in my way will be killed, like all others who do so! Lay down your weapons and return to your ships!"

It was a gutsy approach, but he could only hope his fearful reputation might mean something. Not one of the marines had even raised a weapon to fight back. They had no will to fight. Taylor could see they were utterly demoralised by the war already and had no willpower to fight.

"Turn and walk away is all I ask!"

He holstered his pistol and let the marine go.

"Thank you," the man replied, "We will not interfere."

Taylor watched as they turned and left with weapons still in hand. It gave him hope that humanity might yet unite once again.

"How on Earth did you pull that off?" asked Grey.

"Some of us have it, Captain, and some of us don't," he replied smugly. "Come on, let's move."

They knew where to go now, and Taylor was rushing through the corridors and ramps without any concern for his own safety. Herbert was starting to wonder if anything mattered to him in life besides their Regiment.

"You know what he did back on that defence platform?"

he asked Grey.

"I got some idea. Doesn't sound smart to me, but what do I know? I wasn't there, and I didn't know the options he faced. Have faith in the Colonel. He's seen us through this far."

"It's not faith in the Colonel I lack; it's faith in our ability to handle what's coming next."

"What do you mean?"

"Erdogan."

Grey's face turned to stone at the name.

"You saw him?"

"A hologram, yes."

"Then he's here, and we're in deep shit."

Grey spoke nothing more of it, knowing they must focus on the task at hand, but he could not let the feeling go at the back of his mind that they were in for a world of hurt like they had never known before.

Erdogan? Taylor thought. *How could we ever be so stupid to think he wouldn't come for us? If Earth is really the paradise they seek, why would they not come?*

Shadows appeared ahead of them, and it made Taylor tighten his grip on his rifle. He stopped for a moment and took aim, but the figures continued to run towards him. He could see no weapons. Then they came into view, and he could see it was two pairs of medics. They were carrying stretchers with wounded. He looked down and both casualties were German marines. It brought a little smirk to his face, as he knew who was the cause. But it soon dissipated when he thought of the casualties their own side must have suffered.

They passed on through corridor after corridor and descended many levels until they heard gunfire. They knew they were getting close. Taylor just prayed there were enough left to save.

"Stop right there!" a voice boomed.

He could see an officer at the head of a platoon.

Don't make me do this.

His own battle-hardened troops were far better armoured than their opponents and quickly took up positions. Taylor sighed; he was wary of announcing his presence and not getting the response he wanted, but he thought it was worth a chance one last time.

"I am Colonel Taylor of the Inter-Allied Regiment, European Alliance. You are ordered to stand down!"

"Taylor? We've been fighting Taylor the last hour, so who the hell are you?"

The officer stepped forward to address him and looked down at his uniform with Jones' name.

"What kind of trick are you playing here, Captain? Taylor is in there, and it's our job to capture him, alive if possible."

Taylor could see the man was a Captain of the Nassau's Marine detachment. He was now looking with more interest at Taylor's nametag.

"Captain…Jones. You are with them. You are under arrest. Lay down your weapons!"

"Listen to me!"

"There is nothing to listen to, Captain. You are under arrest!"

"Arrest? This is a war, you fucking idiot. You ain't arresting AWOL idiots."

"Take aim!" ordered the Marine Captain.

Without hesitation, Taylor ripped his pistol from its holster and fired three shots from muscle memory. The room went silent again, and all they could hear was the distant gunfire. The Captain fell forward into his arms, and he lowered him to the floor. A few shots were fired from the German side, and Taylor could do nothing but lift his shield and wait it out while his own side returned fire. Gunfire zipped back and forth for two minutes until all was silent once again, and he got to his feet.

"Why?" he asked himself. "Why fight back now? It's over."

The German marines had been cut down where they stood, but their presence had gained attention, and more troops were flooding towards them from another corridor. Taylor turned back to his own people.

"I never wanted to kill a human in these wars, but by God I will not let a single man stand before us and those we care for. Follow me!"

He rushed towards the sound of the incoming troops,

and as they came into sight, he could see they were a mix of German marines and Mechs, but it did not slow down his pace. He drove his shield forward, and with Assegai in hand strode at the enemy without any fear at all.

Shots ricocheted from the shield, and he was in amongst the enemy within seconds. He was in his element now. He was fighting to save Jones and Parker, and all those he cared about, and nothing would stop him. He barged the first with his shoulder so hard, the man was thrown into the two at his back. Taylor ducked under the next rifle before him and drove his Assegai up through the man's armour.

His shield drove up against a Mech, forcing it back against the sidewall of the corridor and thrusting three times into its torso. He stepped past it, and it dropped down dead behind him. Grey and the others were not far behind and cut their way through their attackers as if there was no resistance at all.

When Taylor finally reached the last soldier of the column, he drove his Assegai deep into the man's stomach, and he collapsed onto the Colonel's shoulder. It was only with this last death he finally realised what they had done. The man dropped from him and slumped down dead. He told himself it was necessary to defend those he loved, but it didn't make him feel any easier.

"Come on, we aren't far away now," said Grey.

Taylor looked down as his hands. They were covered in

red blood, human blood. He could smell the iron of the blood mixed with the salt of his own sweat. He'd tasted his own blood more often than he would like, and it never tasted good. He felt a hand at his back; someone was dragging him along. Herbert was at his side.

"We're almost there now, Colonel."

He started to walk under his own power and understood what he was saying.

Parker, he thought. She was close now; he could feel it. They took a turn ahead to find they were at the back of a defensive wall of German marines.

"What should we do?" Grey asked.

The marines were still oblivious to their presence and clearly trying to deal with the hellish situation Jones had created for them.

"Kill them all," he ordered.

Automatic gunfire opened up. The marines were cut down where they stood until the last few lay own their weapons to surrender and were given mercy. Taylor stepped forward to their position without any care for his life at all. He turned his comms onto the tannoy and yelled out for everyone to hear.

"This is Colonel Taylor of the Inter-Allied Regiment. This fight is over. Lay down your weapons, and no further harm will come to you."

With that, he stepped over the barricade and towards the defenders. Many of them stood up in amazement at him striding towards them.

"Can't be," one of them muttered.

Then he found Parker. Her left arm was in a sling and her face bloody from shrapnel. Tears came to her eyes as she spotted him. He ignored all others and leapt over them, taking her in his arms.

"You're alive. I can't believe you're alive," she whispered in his ear.

"Made it, you dog."

Taylor turned around, and there was Jones. He had glancing wounds on both arms, a bandage wrapped around his head, and blood trickling down one leg, but he was still on his feet.

"You're gonna need a new set of BDUs," he stated.

"I figured as much."

He looked around at the dozens of dead and wounded around them, some their own and others enemy who had gotten into hand-to-hand. A mound of dead Mechs formed an improvised barricade on one flank.

"Did you do it? Did you disable the weapons?"

"Sure did, Eli."

He looked over to one flank where German soldiers battling from a corridor had stood up with their weapons lowered.

"It's over!" Taylor shouted.

"What now?"

"Get to the bridge, Parker, and let the World and this

fleet know the deal."

Jafar strode up and joined the group.

"Still alive as well, you ugly bastard?" asked Taylor.

He seemed confused, not understanding the humour.

"Met a few of your sort aboard that thing. When I could have done with you most, you were not there."

"On your orders," he replied sternly.

Taylor could not disagree.

"Come on, let's end this for good."

He headed for the bridge. Ten of his unit, including Jones and Parker followed, while the rest stayed and took care of the wounded. As they strode through the ship, not a single one of the crew dared intervene. They were covered in dirt and blood, theirs, other humans, and alien. They looked liked death itself rolling through the battleship.

They finally reached the bridge and found two guards on duty in pristine uniforms. They reached for their weapons, but Taylor hollered in a booming voice, "Don't even think about it!"

It was enough to make them stop at the terrifying sight. Jafar standing at Taylor's side was what topped it off and make them think twice.

"Stop him!" A voice shouted from inside the bridge.

Taylor stepped aboard. A German Admiral was frantically looking around the room and expecting someone to act on his order. He wanted to say something but could not find the words.

"I am commandeering this vessel in the name of the European Alliance. I am Colonel Taylor, and you will consider me Captain of this vessel and Commander of the fleet. The Admiral is to be detained immediately!"

Herbert stepped forward and obliged. Nobody said a word as Taylor stepped up to the communications officer.

"Get me a direct line to here," he said, showing the man the codes on his Mappad. The officer looked fearful but did as ordered. A few moments later, General Dupont appeared to them in his own quarters. His head was lowered into his hands, and it was clear he had been waiting for a call for sometime. He looked up in surprise at the bloody Taylor and his comrades who stood before him.

"Taylor? What the hell is going on up there? I am told you destroyed the Earth Defence Grid?"

"Long story, General. Short one, it had to be done."

Dupont shook his head, knowing there was nothing that could be done now.

"I have taken command of the Nassau and ordered its crew to stand down. The fleet should do the same shortly."

Dupont opened his mouth to speak, but the signal cut out and went to static.

"Where the hell did he go?" asked Taylor.

"I'm getting interference, Sir."

"Well sort it!"

The room went silent for a moment before the XO

piped up.

"Colonel, we've got incoming. Lots of them!"

Taylor rushed to his side. There were dozens and dozens of artefacts on the scanner, and not far from Earth.

"What are those?"

"Ships, and not ours."

"We've got an incoming transmission!" the comms officer said.

"From who?"

"Unverified, no idea, Sir."

He was abruptly interrupted by a hologram appearing in the middle of the bridge, and Taylor's heart sank. It was Erdogan.

"I am Lord Erdogan. I am here to claim Earth in the name of the Krycenaean people. Lay down your weapons, and you will not be harmed. Fight, and you will die."

The transmission ended. Taylor knew a war was upon them at the weakest point humanity had been in a hundred years.

How on Earth can we win now when we are divided and weak?

"That's it, Mitch?" asked Parker. "No deals? No negotiations?"

"Hey, at least he's honest," replied Taylor.

"More than we got from his predecessors," added Herrera.

The room went quiet, everyone speculating as to what it could mean.

"Can you get me an open message to the fleet? This one and the EA?" he asked.

The comms officer nodded. "What's left of this fleet, yes, Sir."

"Do it!"

"You're on," he replied.

Taylor coughed, not expecting it to happen quite so quickly as it did.

"You all know who I am," he began. "Recently, we have fought one another; the reasons of which no longer matter. You heard what Erdogan had to say. He wants Earth for himself. Will you stand by and let that happen, or will you fight for what is rightfully ours? Stand with me. Let our fleets stand together and end this while we can. Erdogan is the greatest among them, so this can be the end of these wars forever!"

He took a deep breath, thinking about his next words.

"Those who would fight form up beside the Nassau and fight alongside us. Those who would not, leave now and take no further part in this."

He gestured for the officer to end the transmission and hoped for the best. Parker leaned in close and whispered to him. "What do you know about ship combat?"

He shrugged. "I don't know what to do other than fight."

"Weapon systems, what have we got?"

"Still trying to restore power, Sir. Systems are minimal

at best."

"Fighters?"

"At a quarter capacity."

"Launch everything we've got."

Taylor knew they were already facing a losing battle.

"Let's see what we're facing. Put it on screen."

A projection flashed up, and they could see a vessel several kilometres wide that was ten times that in length. It was an ugly vessel, with the aerodynamics of a brick, and yet more intimidating than most of what any of them had ever seen. It reminded Taylor of the K'til that he had fought so hard to destroy. More warships than he could count surrounded it.

"What can we do against this but lay down and die?" asked the comms officer.

Taylor resented his negativity but understood where he was coming from. The distance was closing rapidly now, and all Taylor could do was pray for a miracle. He turned to Jones for some snippet of advice, but he could see the look of loss in the Captain's eyes. It was hopeless, and they all knew it.

Fighters swarmed out in front of them as a number of vessels joined them, and the EA fleet approached their flank.

It's not enough, not near enough.

He thought back to the first time Erdogan had appeared to him and Herbert and wondered if it had all been for nothing with this new enemy.

If we barely survived the previous wars, how can we win against the greatest of the alien Lords?

They were questions he had no answers to.

Lights flashed on the screen, and two of the smaller vessels ahead were blown apart. The crew watched as the enemy vessels hammered the fleet with beam weapons and pulses, and without any noticeable return from their own side. A pulse from the capitol ship soared towards them, and a few of the crew screamed for someone to do something, but there was nothing they could do. It ripped into the hull of the Nassau and was followed by three more impacts. A siren sounded out as emergency lighting flashed.

"We've got breaches on twelve floors, and we're losing power!"

He saw several other lights zoom towards them at a slower velocity and crash into the hull.

"What the hell was that?"

"Boarding craft," Jafar said calmly.

"We've got enemy combatants on board. Alert all marines to sweep and clear!"

He picked up his shield and rushed to the door. He stopped beside one of the marines standing guard as they passed by and tore his rifle away from him.

"Give me that!"

The man barely put up a fight as Taylor took it from

him and carried on down the corridor.

"Do you even know where you're going?" asked Parker.

"One of those breaches hit forward of here about two floors up, and we're gonna do what we do best."

He stopped and put his hand up to her chest to stop her in her tracks.

"You're wounded. I'm not gonna stop you coming, but you stay at the back, you hear?"

She grunted.

"Did you hear me, Sergeant?" he bellowed, desperately.

The breach was just one of the many problems facing them, but at least it was one he could deal with. They rushed down a ramp to a level where they could already hear gunfire. They found two of the crew carrying one of their wounded. They pointed back in the direction they were coming from. Taylor carried on with his weapons held at the ready. He'd been fighting humans and their Mech allies for so long, he was looking forward to getting stuck into the real deal.

Pulses flashed up ahead, and Taylor rushed right for them. Jafar and Jones were beside him. One of the pulses struck his shield, and he was relieved to feel it be absorbed as they were intended to do, and he carried on without noticing the blast. He fired on full auto, emptying twenty or more shots into the first Mech in utter overkill. He didn't even release the trigger and simply panned the weapon across to turn it on the next.

The magazine ran dry, and Taylor quickly let go of the rifle and drew out his Assegai. It was still coated in dry blue blood that began melting as the weapon quickly heated up. He approached the first Mech, dropped down, and slid on his knees until he reached it. His shield drove high into the Mech's weapon and his Assegai drove into its groin.

He pulled out the weapon, spun around at a tremendous speed, and drove it into the next; and then smashed the other off its feet with his shield. Taylor felt like he was back in the last war. It felt good, remembering what he was fighting for, but as he drove his Assegai into the last Mech soldier still standing, he was overwhelmed at how empty he now felt.

The enemy he had always been warned about was upon them, and it was beginning to feel like the first day of the first invasion all over again. He cast his eyes around to see that between them they had cut down twelve Mechs for the loss of one of their unit.

"You okay, Mitch?" Jones asked.

He didn't even notice the question.

"You okay?" screamed Jones.

He wasn't. His confidence and cool-headedness was gone. His head was spinning like it would after a few dozen beers, and he was feeling just as sick. Jones shook him and finally punched him on the nose. It was a shock enough to make him snap out of it.

"You need to get back to the bridge. We need you

there!" he pleaded.

Jones turned to Jafar.

"Take him back to the bridge, and Parker, you go with him!"

There was no more debate to be had, and Taylor obliged. Jafar grabbed his shoulder and hauled him off like a little school kid, with Parker following close behind.

"Erdogan, he came to me as a hologram before."

"What did he say to you?" asked Jafar.

"Does it matter? We know why he's here. He's here to take this world, and we're powerless to stop him. We're a crippled race just waiting to be mopped up."

"What about the defence grid?"

"Nothing left of it, Eli. We destroyed it."

"You what!"

He understood now. Erdogan was not the egocentric power hungry fool he had faced before, but a very smart and calculating one. He never had a choice between his friends and his planet. He had but one choice, and Erdogan had made it for him.

"Goddamn it," he muttered to himself.

They stepped back onto the bridge, and all attention was now turned to him. Despite being his enemy until moments before, they now looked to him as the miracle worker and saviour he had a reputation of being. He strolled onto the bridge in a stunned state with blue blood still trickling from his weapon.

He looked around and could see the crew wanted answers from him, but he had none.

"What do we do, Colonel?" asked the XO.

Taylor didn't even respond; he knew it was over. Another two impacts ripped through the ship, and they were being pulled into the Earth's atmosphere. They were losing power. They were already dangerously close from when the EMP had first struck.

"We're going down, mayday, mayday, mayday!"

Taylor didn't say a word, for he knew there was nothing more he could do. He turned to Parker and wished they could survive it, if only he could have another day with her. The panic of the crew around them came to a silence as the battleship began to burn up in the atmosphere. The fact they now only had the atmosphere to contend with and not Erdogan's fleet at least brought some relief.

"Escape pods?" Taylor cried out, almost begging.

"We've lost half of them, and most of the others haven't got enough power to launch," replied the XO.

"Then what do we do?"

"Hope for the best, Colonel. Hope for the best."

It was the answer he was expecting but not the one he wanted to hear. As they passed through the atmosphere, the camera views all around them showed nothing but flames and chunks of the hull that were torn from the ship. They could see the odd crewmember sucked out from breaches and were at least safe in the knowledge they were at the core of the vessel.

Taylor was sitting on the floor and felt Parker crawl up to him. Tears were streaming from her eyes. It was a horrible sight, worse than anything he had seen that day.

"We're gonna make it, Mitch. We have to. We can't die here," she insisted.

She was the only reason he wanted to live, and that alone was enough for him to get himself to his feet.

"What power do we have left?" he asked.

"Not a lot!" yelled the XO. "Everything we have is going to the landing thrusters to slow our speed."

"Negative, put all power to the engines, and get our nose up!"

"Sir, we haven't got enough power to get us back in the air!"

"Just do it!"

"I will not!"

"We cannot slow our speed enough to safely hit the ground, so we need to skim the water," Taylor said calmly, but with stern authority.

"Skim the water? We'll hit it like a brick."

"Raise the bow. All power to engines!"

"This isn't a copter, Colonel. It's a battleship. Sir!" he pleaded.

Taylor drew out his pistol, rushed across the bridge, and grabbed the XO by the head. He had no idea if his crazy plan had any chance of working. All he knew is their current trajectory would result in certain death.

"Do it now!" he demanded.

"You'll kill us all!" cried the XO.

Taylor fired without any hesitation. The bullet passed through the XO's head and blood sprayed out across the bridge. He went limp and collapsed to the floor. He turned his pistol on the next crewmember he could see.

"Lift the bow, and put all other power to the engines!"

The crew quickly obliged, and they felt the ship soar forward.

There's life in the old girl yet, he told himself.

Further warning lights flashed on the flight console, and a voice rang out. "Warning, collision imminent! Warning, collision imminent."

"No shit," Taylor muttered to himself.

The bow was beginning to rise, and they had got over the Atlantic, but they were still plummeting like a brick. Taylor told himself they were going to make it. They were going to make it because he wanted another day with Parker, and because he didn't risk it all not to save her and Jones and all the others.

He turned to look back at her. Parker was sitting against the Captain's chair and holding on tight. A smile came to her face when she saw him looking back at her. Taylor had felt helpless many times throughout the wars, but never so much as now when he could literally do nothing more to affect their survival.

"I love you, Eli!" he called out, barely loud enough for her to hear.

A moment later they crashed into the ocean and were thrown off their feet. Taylor smashed into the ceiling of the bridge and was just conscious enough to feel the impact as he once again hit the floor. As he felt blood trickle down from his skull, he could only think of the mountain that lay before them. He couldn't tell if he was dead, dying, or just stunned, but as he passed out, he had one thought.

Now we're in the shit.